DOWNRANGE

A Novel By
Andrew Layton

MARSHALL - MICHIGAN
800PUBLISHING.COM

Downrange

Copyright © 2012 by Andrew Layton

Layout by Kait Lamphere

Author photo courtesy of author

The opinions expressed in this manuscript are solely the opinions of the author and do not represent the opinions or thoughts of the publisher. The author represents and warrants that s/he either owns or has the legal right to publish all material in this book.

ISBN-13: 978-1-938110-36-8

First published in 2012

10 9 8 7 6 5 4 3 2 1

Published by   2 MOON PRESS
123 W. Michigan Ave, Marshall, Michigan 49068
www.800publishing.com

All Rights Reserved. This book may not be reproduced, transmitted, or stored in whole or in part by any means, including graphic, electronic, or mechanical without the express written consent of the publisher except in the case of brief quotations embodied in critical articles and reviews.

PRINTED IN THE UNITED STATES OF AMERICA

FOR ELISE

Author's Note

It must be made clear that although the motivation for writing this book has been fueled purely by experience, the characters, situations and places contained within are entirely fiction. This story does not document the day-to-day events of a deployment as they actually occurred, nor was it written in order to embellish the idea of being in Iraq or Afghanistan. It was written simply in hopes of capturing some of the sights, sounds and feelings that defined life for me, and hopefully for some of those I served with, "downrange."

ALSO BY THE AUTHOR

Wolverines in the Sky:
Michigan's Fighter Aces of WWI, WWII and Korea

Eagles' Wings: An Uncommon Story of World War II

1

As the wheels of the C-130 cargo plane deployed with a lurch, Staff Sergeant David Holman closed his eyes and tried to ignore the clawing pain that shot through his body as his back chafed against the forty pounds of body armor slung over it. He was embarking upon his second combat deployment to the Middle East in three years and the next ground he'd walk upon would be war-zone Iraqi ground. He wondered to himself if he was truly ready for it.

He'd worked hard to position himself for this deployment - he was a reservist, and he had volunteered for this opportunity out of a conviction to once again be a part of something larger than himself. He'd felt an unnamed yet intoxicating fulfillment during the six months he had spent in Afghanistan – or at least he remembered it that way – and it was to quench his brewing thirst for more of that curious gratification that had driven him to step forward once again.

Now, when the only thing left between him and the war were the rubber wheels of the landing gear and a few feet of concrete, he wasn't sure. He rubbed his eyes, blinked, and wondered to himself if the weight he felt over his body was from the bullet-proof armor or the thought of another one hundred and eighty-three days in this mess.

It had already required a grueling trip to get to this

point. It had begun four days earlier at a regional airport in Michigan when he'd said goodbye to his bride of six months and climbed onto the commercial airliner feeling remarkably disoriented. She had taken his departure quite well, he thought. That is, up until the last moment when she pulled her hand away from David after their last kiss and turned away – as if to turn her back on the reality of his leaving. That was his final memory of her before he turned and boarded the plane, and it sat in the pit of his stomach like a burning coal as he shifted uncomfortably into his seat. He remembered the sweetness of that final kiss. "No," he thought. "I can't dwell on that now." He pushed the thoughts of Kristine to the back of his mind and told himself to focus on his surroundings and the adventure that was about to unfold.

The commercial airliner had been hot and stuffy on that early September day. Taking in the images of the half-empty plane, the sad-eyed flight attendant pushing her refreshment cart and the fraying headrest of the seat in front of him, David had been struck by the irony of it all. "This isn't a very dignified way to go to war," he thought to himself. Alone. Economy seating, "Peanuts or cookie, sir?" The old lady sitting next to David interrupted his thoughts. She had seen the "U.S. AIRFORCE" patch embroidered on his fatigues and asked him what kind of plane he flew, intrigued by his uniform. Annoyed by her ignorance, he informed her politely that not everyone in the Air Force is a pilot. She turned away, her interest disbursing as rapidly as it had gathered. She didn't even ask where he was headed, which was a relief to David.

After making a connection stop in Detroit, David landed at Baltimore International Airport, a major hub of contracted military air transport. Fumbling his way through the ticketing and administrative procedures, he learned that he was to depart on an overseas flight with several hundred other deploying service members the next morning. "Nice," he said out loud when he saw the itinerary – Ramstein, Germany; Aviano, Italy; and finally Al Udeid, Qatar. From there, He'd pick up a C-130 or C-17 sortie into his final destination, a forward operating base in Iraq.

As David shoved his already crumpled orders back into his pocket, a lady in her sixties, passing out ice cream sandwiches, stopped him and suggested God's blessing upon his travels. He turned, said "Thank you," and began munching on the frozen sandwich, figuring that it would pass for dinner. It was only 6:00pm, but David Holman was tired from the day's traveling. He checked into the airport's USO lounge for the night. He found a comfortable-looking sofa and leaned back, trying to relax as much as possible. As soon as he tried to close his eyes, David's mind began twitching back and forth, alternately fixating on revived images from his first deployment and the looming unknown of what was ahead. The 37 marines cooped around him with their luggage didn't help, either. He barely slept at all.

The next twenty-four hours passed in a blur and before he knew it, David was at a Bavarian hotel in Kaiserslauten, Germany. The civilian contract plane he'd left Baltimore on had struck a flock of birds while on descent into Ramstein Air Base and was declared unflyable by the maintenance crews. The Air Force, normally not prone to fancy quartering, was left with no choice but to deposit the two hundred or so passengers into a nearby hotel while an unlucky logistics officer scrambled for an aircraft. The passengers high-fived as they all packed into one gigantic bus, knowing they'd been handed a taxpayer-funded night on the town. The German driver floored it as they tore down the autobahn and weaved the bus in and out of traffic to make good time. Arriving at their hotel, the paying guests stared in amazement as a herd of uniformed Americans debarked, slapping each other on the back with enthusiasm and confirming over and over again to one another what a great deal they had lucked into. David didn't know another soul on that bus, but as he looked at the smiles worn by the other airmen around him, he felt an unmistakable kinship with them. A smile cracked his own lips as he considered his good fortune.

The travelers automatically filed into a line and waited patiently as the proprietor handed out the keys to their suites. The man, an older, gaunt German said in halting but proud English that it would have to be three men to a room. Standing behind David was a young Airman 1st Class with a smile on his face and eyes full of excitement. He introduced himself as Jack Doolittle and struck up a friendly conversation. He was a good talker and spoke with enthusiasm.

"This is my first deployment," he said. "How about you?"

David took in the young man's fresh face and smiled. "Number two." Jack nodded and asked David where he was headed.

"A little FOB north of Baghdad."

"It's not called Sherman, is it?"

"Yes."

"No way, I think I'm going there, too."

"Well, we'll be seeing plenty of each other then; I don't think it's a very big place." They agreed to crash in the same room but needed a third man to get their key from the desk. Another Staff Sergeant stood near them; he was sulking over something and didn't appear to be thrilled at their magnanimous gesture when David offered him an in. "Can't sleep in the lobby," he muttered to no one in particular as they shuffled down the hall. David and Jack never did get his name.

The suites that they were assigned were more than comfortable. Jack tried out both beds and inspected the equally impressive bathroom. He had traveled in the United States before, but this introduction to world travel was really suiting him well so far. He would soon find out that the best part of the evening was yet to come – the meal tickets. Along with their keys, all of the transient airmen had been given three meal coupons from a restaurant located just across the street. Starving after a twelve-hour plane ride and nothing to eat since the previous night, Jack and David threw their bags on the floor of the hotel room and ventured out into the cool evening to see if they could get some food. The Sulking Sergeant, as the two airmen quickly named their roommate, distained their company, preferring to sit in a corner until they left.

The September air was damp with drizzle and David didn't have a coat except for his ABU fatigue top, so he ran across the street as quickly as he could. A neon Bittberger sign lit up the sidewalk in front of a café and a covered porch extended along the building's side. The name of the place didn't make an impression on David's memory, but he stepped inside, ducking, so as not to hit his head on a potted plant that hung dangerously low into the walkway. Then he looked into the warm room, which held about five dozen hungry servicemen sitting around tables loaded with schnitzel, sausage, and warm bread. Most were guzzling steins of pitch-black locally brewed beer.

Jack found the two of them seats at a table with a few other airmen. As soon as he sat down, a blonde waitress asked in broken English what he wanted. "I'll have that," David said, pointing to a photo of schnitzel and potatoes on the menu. As quickly as she had appeared, she was gone again and Jack turned around to watch her glide back into the kitchen.

As they waited for their food, the others at their table, four in all, introduced themselves. They were all part of a C-130 crew that was heading to Balad, Iraq. The crewmember sitting next to David stuck out his hand. He had a crooked nose and spoke with a Texas drawl. "Chance Spillman," he said. David replied to make the introduction complete and the two engaged in polite small talk until their food arrived.

Jack tried to keep up with their conversation but was distracted by the atmosphere. It struck him in a peculiar way that he was amidst a group of men who were actually heading off to war. He had read about stuff like this in the context of World War II and Vietnam, but now this was real and he was actually living it. To him, it felt as if he was on the verge of a great adventure and the excitement that was generated by that thought hung so thick in the room that he just sat there gulping it all in with big, energetic drafts that seemed to make his lungs want to burst with anticipation.

The pretty waitress interrupted Jack's thoughts and smiled at him, placing a tray of food on the table. David glanced away from his conversation with the flyers as his food arrived as well. "That was fast," he remarked.

Meanwhile, Jack's eyes bulged at the frothing stein of black beer that towered over the rest of the meal. He thanked the waitress before she disappeared again, this time brushing Jack's shoulder with her fingertips as she turned away. Feeling embarrassed, he managed a sheepish smile before taking a few bites of the well-seasoned meat. He reached for the stein to wash it down and took a small, cautious sip. At twenty, Jack would still be under legal drinking age in the states but to his delight Germany's liberalized alcohol policy erased that statute that he'd always tried to adhere to. When the brew hit his tongue, he nearly spat it back out. Apparently, a taste for German beer was something Jack had yet to acquire.

For the rest of meal, the table was silent as the men focused on potatoes and schnitzel. By the end, the beer was starting to taste better to Jack and he finished the entire stein with great satisfaction. David had been watching the younger man intently. There was something magnetic about his enthusiasm, yet the boy seemed aloof.

"I don't think you ever mentioned where you were from."

Jack blurted out his reply. "Jacksonville, Florida."

"Nice. You have any family?"

"Not really, just my mom and dad."

"So what made you want to join this Air Force?"

"Don't really know; just to do something different, I guess."

"Are you guard, reserve, or active?"

"Active."

Jack's eyes were still flashing around the dining room and David could tell that he didn't want to chat. Chance had by now wandered outside for a smoke with the rest of the C-130 crew. David nodded his head toward the door. "Well?" he asked. Jack nodded; his senses numbed by the pleasant haze of alcohol, and they both rose from the table and walked back out into the mist.

They had almost made it to their hotel suite where David planned on crashing for a healthy sleep when they ran into Chance, who was sitting in the courtyard outside of what was apparently their window, puffing on a cigar with his feet up on a table. "Hey," he called, "come have a seat." Jack sat down next to him and didn't say anything. Chance began to talk, which he was good at. David listened as he talked about everything he could think of, his wife, his two kids, and his first car. Jack listened as well, but was soon thinking of other things. He watched the cigar smoke trail upwards into the night sky and wondered if there was a full moon behind those damp clouds. Sitting there, a long way from home, Jack suddenly felt that it would be a great comfort to see the moon. His mind flashed back to a summer vacation when his parents took to the Atlantic coast. He was about nine years old. They had sat on the beach and watched that same moon reflect its light off the far-away waves.

Too homesick to listen to Chance's stories any longer, he excused himself and fumbled his way inside the hotel and walked back up to their third-floor room. The overwhelming excitement that he'd felt at dinner had been replaced by something different. He swung the door of his room open and nearly tripped over the carcass of the Sulking Sergeant. Jack had forgotten about him until just then. It looked like he'd gotten his meal ticket's allotment of beer, plus a little extra. Drunk as a skunk. David came in a few minutes later. "Hey, are you all right?" he asked, as Jack lay down on the couch. The younger man said nothing.

David looked at the two twin-sized beds and asked if Jack intended to use one of them. Jack gestured a negative reply. David pushed the two narrow beds together and sprawled out across them both. Soon, the anxiety and excitement had all melted away and the next thing David knew, it was light outside.

By lunchtime, word had spread that the replacement airliner had arrived back at the base and the bus would soon be at the hotel to pick them all up. David had already packed up his gear and was waiting with Chance and a few others outside the hotel. The sun was out and the clouds that had shrouded the heavens the night before had cleared up. Jack grabbed his bags, too, and waited with the others until the bus showed up. They all piled on again and the same German-speaking driver took the wheel as the bus traced the autobahn back to Ramstein. The plane was waiting for them on the flight line and the airmen boarded meekly, some of them still feeling the strength of the German brews from the night before. David got a seat towards the front of the plane while Jack got stuck way in the back. Between them was a sea of camouflaged bodies that were soon reclined in various positions of unconsciousness as they rode out the journey.

Jack fell asleep to the lull of the aircraft's engines and awoke several hours later to a stunning view from the window on his right side. They were on descent over Italy and the terrain was luscious and green. The sun, partially obscured by cloud cover, seemed to be transmitting rays in every direction, which in turn bounced off of the lingering clouds in vibrant shades of gold and burgundy. Below this spectacle, the lights of Italian villages could easily be seen as they dotted the green countryside, looking much like the fireflies of summer. The fireflies kept growing larger until Jack could make out the actual buildings from which their glow was transmitted. Then they were on the ground, getting off the plane amidst the buildings that made up Aviano Air Base.

It was just past dusk now and flight line workers with flashlights in their hands stood on the tarmac, spaced every so often so that they formed a makeshift pathway leading to a very large hanger. The way they herded the airmen across the flight line when they got off the plane reminded Jack of the way sheep are shepherded in and out of their pens. The transients walked between them and were directed into the huge bay area where cots and ready-to-eat meals had been laid out for the travelers. They'd be spending the night here while their plane was refueled and the crew rested.

Having slept so much of the way here, Jack wasn't too tired and he wandered around the hanger for most of the night. He'd lost David in the shuffle of getting off the plane, which was too bad because he felt like talking to someone to pass time. A broad-shouldered Technical Sergeant was also pacing the length of the hanger. Jack noticed earlier that he wore the career-field occupational badge of a Command Post Controller, which was the same as his own. He approached the Sergeant and asked him where he was going. Soon, the two men established that their destinations were the same – FOB Sherman.

The Sergeant smiled a big toothy grin that made his face look like it was twisted unnaturally out of shape. "Well, you'll probably be one of my troops, then. I'm gonna be the Non-commissioned Officer in Charge of the Command Post section up there." He said his name was Cliff Hartman. He was from North Carolina but was now stationed in England and had been assigned to Jack and David's plane as it departed from Germany. Jack gave him his brief biographical sketch and they waited out the night together before they were herded back onto the plane.

At the next stop, Al Udeid, Qatar, they were finally dropped off for good by the contracted commercial airliners. A major logistics processing center for all Air Force assets heading in or out of the Iraqi combat theater, some of their bunch would stay here for the duration of their deployment and others like Doolittle and Holman would be shipped off yet again via military airlift to various forward operating locations.

As Jack Doolittle walked down the stairs from the aircraft to the pavement, he was hit instantly by the heat - and the smell. For a moment, he thought that surely he was walking around in an industrial-sized oven. At its peak, the sun was absolutely brutal and the humidity from the nearby Persian Gulf was decimating to human energy at any time of the day. The average high for this time of year was just over 130 degrees Fahrenheit and this was an above average day. To go along with the oppressive heat, the place had an unearthly smell that seemed to permeate every one of the thousands of small white rocks that had been spread over most of the base's real estate to keep the dust from blowing around. This dirty, oily odor made the stench of hot trash seem like it would be an improvement. "Get used to it," said David. "This is the land of unusual smells."

Immediately after David and Jack got off the plane, they collected their bags and headed off to the processing center for transient personnel. They were already drenched with sweat. Cliff Hartman was tagging along with them now as well, and he was especially struggling with his weapons case. It was identical to Jack's, except it lacked the wheels and handle that allowed for easy maneuvering. Hartman had the general posture and stride of a jovial ape to begin with, but now the sweat that poured from his nose and forehead made him look especially animate. When he wasn't cursing to himself, his prominent jawbone hung from his face with fatigue as he trudged across the white stone pathway. The blinding sun split into a million sparks of sharp light on every one of the tiny rocks, which made Jack want to punch whoever had put them there.

When they finally got to the processing center (PERSCO, in military lingo), they were told that their flight into Iraq, a C-130 sortie, would leave the next afternoon. In the meantime, they had twenty-four hours to kill. Their temporary quarters would be in one of the large tents that had been set up to accommodate transients who were waiting for flights; other than this concession to sleep they were on their own. A sign in the PERSCO building indicated a base pool and Jack figured that looked as promising as anything. The tent that they would be occupying was really a huge, open-bay cloth barracks that contained about forty sets of bunk beds. Jack and the two sergeants threw their bags on the floor and claimed their bunks. A noisy generator provided rudimentary central air for the tent.

David Holman sat down on one of the mattresses and began unlacing his combat boots. Jack looked at him and sighed. "Enough of this trudging around. I'm going to the pool; want to come?" David looked up and ran his hand through his sweaty hair. "Nahh. I think I'll stay in the air conditioning and read for a bit."

"All right, but you never want to live it up, you know that? You're an old man."

David smiled and waved the airman off. As the door of the tent slammed behind Jack, David leaned back on the bare mattress, pulled an old Hemingway novel out of the pocket of his cargo pants and opened the cover.

That night, the tent was filled with Jack's moans as he nursed his charred skin. He was paying a hefty price for his afternoon at the pool with 130 degrees of sunny heat bearing down on him. Cliff Hartman had taken the bottom bunk, which left Jack with no choice but the top. His attempts to climb up were pitifully slow, but ultimately successful. David was already asleep in his bunk on the other side of the tent. Jack dozed off, despite being aware of Hartman's loping around the tent with his distinctive shuffle. Jack paid him no mind until a rustling of fabric was followed by a gasp.

"You alright?" asked Jack.

"Yeah, everything's fine. I just forgot about my tattoo."

Hartman didn't take the time to explain that he had paid a visit to an English tattoo parlor a few days prior to shipping out to have a giant purple dragon emblazoned across his chest. Spotting this new ink that he was unaccustomed to seeing as he took his shirt off for the night had apparently caused the scare. Jack rolled back onto his mattress, wincing at the twinge of pain caused by his significant sunburn. He wondered what kind of a guy Hartman was – this man he'd be serving under once they got to Iraq.

When the time came to depart the next day, Holman, Hartman and Doolittle arrived on time at the designated loading spot and found six other Americans who would be joining them on their trip to FOB Sherman. They had all been issued extra gear that morning, including body armor, helmets, and ammunition for the M16 rifles and M9 pistols which they still carried in their bulky cases. Those, combined with the personal bags they had brought from home, made them look like a herd of military pack mules. Within minutes, the C-130 aircraft they would ride the rest of the way taxied up in front of them and the enormous loading ramp was lowered to grant their entry.

The nine shuffled onto the ramp and were swallowed up by the Hercules. The door began closing behind them as quickly as it had opened. They turned around and caught a last glimpse of desert as the door locked into place with the clank of metal on metal. The passengers made themselves as comfortable as possible in the mesh seats that ran along either side of the cargo bay. David Holman looked at Jack, who was sitting next to him. The young man's eyes were wide and tense, but sparkled slightly with the anticipation.

"Ready to go?"

"Are you kidding me?"

David smiled again at Jack's constant enthusiasm. He looked down at his own combat boots, then glanced around the belly of the cramped cargo ship and suddenly didn't feel so sure about himself. He clutched his backpack of personal gear a little tighter, as if it were a life preserver that could keep him from drowning in the choppy waves of whatever happened next.

Meanwhile, Jack Doolittle was taking it all in with a smile on his face. Directly across from him were four stoic men, silent and obviously preoccupied with acute focus. Their rugged appearance and attitude made Jack think they might be from a Special Forces unit. Behind them was an enormous American flag that the plane's flight crew had tacked against the inside of the cargo bay. He thought of the heroes that had fought under that same flag and felt his chest swell a little, a tinge of pride. As the drone of the plane's four turbocharged engines swelled to a defining roar, Jack closed his eyes and the next thing he knew, they were moving.

It was about a three-hour plane ride from Al Udeid to FOB Sherman, which Jack counted down by the minute on his wristwatch. They had been whirring along in the back of this monster for quite a while. No one had said a word and even if someone had said something, it would have been drowned out by the plane's howling engines. Suddenly, Jack felt the whole plane bank sharply to its side, throwing what seemed like the entire world off its axis. He was now looking straight up into the air towards the four spec-ops guys and could feel the forces of gravity working against the blood circulating in his head. He quickly glanced around the cargo bay and noted that everyone's eyes were bulging with alarm. Cliff Hartman looked over at Jack, his teeth gritted tightly from the g-forces. Then the sensation of a sudden loss of altitude made his stomach want to turn and he thought for a moment that they might be going down.

The wild banking continued for a few more seconds before it turned into a calculated, downward spiral that ended when the plane leveled out and touched down on FOB Sherman's concrete airstrip. They taxied for a few moments and as the engines powered down, David leaned over to Jack and said "What'd ya think of that combat landing?" Jack raised his eyebrows and nodded back in mock approval, attempting to look combat-hardened but still feeling queasy; especially since he knew those antics in the sky were in all likelihood an evasive tactic to avoid small-arms fire from insurgents on the ground.

He didn't linger on this thought for long, for the loading ramp was again being lowered. It revealed a bleak landscape, shrouded by the darkness of an Iraqi night, interrupted only by a couple of floodlights set up along the tarmac. Hartman stood from his mesh seat and grabbed Jack's arm, pulling him up with him. "Let's go," he said, looking at Jack with a sense of urgency. Doolittle scrambled to collect his gear, simultaneously keeping his eye on the rag-tag loading crew that was now rushing up the ramp to help expedite their departure. David followed with his gear in tow. One of the loaders approached Jack, his face goggled like a space alien to protect his eyes from the air forced behind the plane from its propellers, and offered to take his weapons case for him. Jack followed him off the plane and looked around, taking in his first glimpse of Iraq. His momentary observation was interrupted by a long file of blindfolded teenagers, nineteen or twenty of them, being led onto the plane and possibly into the very seats he and the others had just vacated. They were insurgent detainees, captured and now being sent to an unknown location for an unknown purpose. The silent spec-ops troops on the plane had been guards.

The goggled cargo loader threw Jack's weapon case into the back of a white Dodge pickup, turned around, and yelled over the engines, "Welcome to Sherman, bud."

"Thanks, glad to have finally made it."

The goggled trooper looked at the truck and then back at Jack. "I'd help ya with the rest of your bags if you were an officer, but you're not." A huge smile seemed to swallow his face as he climbed into the driver's seat and started the engine. The three airmen threw the rest of their gear into the bed. Jack jumped into the extended cab while David called shotgun. Cliff Hartman squeezed into the jump seat behind the driver. The loader, still wearing his ridiculous goggles, turned and offered them all a vigorous handshake. "The name's Blake Davidson," he said. "Are you guys ready to roll?"

2

Blake wheeled the pickup down the flight line while David Holman watched as shacks of corrugated metal and gigantic tents passed beyond the windshield. He was experiencing his first moments in Iraq, but his mind was in Afghanistan. Memories of his first deployment had been the standard by which he'd mentally primed himself for this trip. Now, what David was seeing was not Afghanistan. The lack of correlation between the two caught him off guard and he shook his head at the realization of how foolish he'd been to believe that there would be any way to compare the two experiences. From that moment on, he was starting from scratch.

The taxiway was sparsely lined with blue runway lights that flickered weakly in the darkness. Cliff Hartman watched them pass by, one by one. They illuminated enough of the concrete for him to observe their dusty working environment for the first time. He leaned closer to Blake.

"It's not much, is it?"

"Nahh, but its home."

Cliff grunted indignantly. "Well, I think I already feel I've been here too long." Blake laughed out loud. "What you've got to do, man, is embrace the suck!" Cliff rolled his eyes as Blake's grin stretched from ear to ear.

Meanwhile, Jack's eyes were bulging at the sight of military equipment in action on the flight line. "I don't know; I think this this is pretty cool," he remarked. "Where do we get out?" He was craning his neck to get a better view of a helicopter parked near the taxiway.

Blake weaved through several intersections of concrete before stopping in front of a decrepit sandstone building and told the three passengers to get out of the truck. "Here ya go boys," he said in his distinctive accent, "Like I was saying, this is your new home away from home."

David Holman lowered himself from the passenger's seat. Holman and Doolittle fell out of the cab. All were still weighed down by their body armor and helmets which added a good forty pounds to the weight of their baggage. Jack looked up to survey the building and could barely believe his eyes. Concrete blast walls had been placed all around the front of the structure and Arabic graffiti was visible on those sections not obscured by the barriers. A small American flag hung from a pole that had been lashed to the side of one of the outer walls with duct tape.

Cliff Hartman looked at Jack with skepticism as he dropped his gear on the ground outside of the blast wall perimeter. "We come all this way to work in a place like this." They both went for the plywood door which appeared to be the building's entrance, walking under a canopy of camouflaged netting in the process. On the wall next to the door, a crude mural of an eagle wielding an enormous bomb in its talons had been slapped onto the sandstone. David Holman stopped to take a closer look at the artwork. He made a mental note to tell Kristine about this later on. They'd always enjoyed visiting historical sites and museums together and this place looked as if it has been witness to a library's worth of history. She would want to know about it.

David pulled open the door and followed Doolittle and Hartman inside a dimly-lit hallway. He immediately noticed that the sandstone walls were scarred with hundreds of divots where machine gun rounds had scarred the building as if it had once had a bad case of chicken pox. Jack Doolittle and Cliff Hartman had stopped in a room off to David's left. He looked in and saw five airmen huddled around a set of radios and a couple of computers. Maps were sprawled and tacked to all four walls surrounding them. They were clearly engrossed in their work and barely acknowledged the new arrivals. Of the five airmen, two were female Staff Sergeants, two were male Senior Airmen and one was a middle-aged Captain. The Captain was the first to look up at them. "Hey, there you are," he said, and rose from his chair to offer a handshake.

"We've been expecting you for a while now. I'm Captain Garrison, and this is the mobility operations center. It looks like you found us all right."

A phone rang behind him. He paused and turned as one of the Staff Sergeants dove to answer it. She took notes vigorously as she listened to the voice on the other end of the line.

Garrison took a deep breath, returned his attention to the new arrivals and continued, "This room is the command post, where you'll be working. This is one of our controllers, Senior Airman Burr, and these are our load planners, Staff Sergeant Shaw, Staff Sergeant Jason and over here is Airman Graham." Each of them nodded and offered a greeting as their names were mentioned.

Garrison was a tall man, about six-foot two and not

quite heavyset. About forty-five or so, his deeply tanned skin was offset by a grey buzz cut. He spoke with an eloquent diction that pegged him as a southerner. Looking at Jack, he asked if Sergeant Davidson had dropped the two of them out front. Again, Jack nodded.

"Well, he'll be the one to show Sergeant Hartman and Sergeant Holman around tonight," he said, turning his eyes to each man as he spoke. For Jack, he had other plans. "Airman Doolittle, you're going directly to work. Sergeant Davidson will get you squared away at your quarters in the morning. Right now, your time belongs to Airman Burr. He's rotating out tomorrow morning and you will be his replacement."

As the two Sergeants followed Blake to their quarters, Jack pulled a chair up to a rickety desk that was weighed down with three computers and a layer of ashy desert dust. Burr said that Jack could skip the formalities and call him Andy. Jack obliged and focused on Burr's words as he gave a brief description of what Jack's duties would entail for the duration of his six month tour. "You're basically Captain Garrison's operational eyes and ears," he said. "Any aircraft that comes into FOB Sherman will radio to you first. Your main job is to coordinate their mission requirements from here, whether that includes handling equipment and load teams to take care of their cargo, or close air support from the Army for combat situations." Jack thought back to the Apache helicopters he had seen sitting along the taxiway earlier that night. Burr also outlined the additional command post duties including distribution and monitoring of the daily flying schedule for FOB Sherman and a periodic situational report officially submitted to higher headquarters to document important happenings at this detached aerial port.

For the rest of the night, Jack sat there with Burr, listening to him talk about his tour of duty and trying to soak up as much information as possible. "You'll get used to the pace," he said. "Time goes by fast when you're always working." After a few hours at the console, Burr offered to show Jack around the place a little more. He agreed and followed Burr down the hallway and out the back door. Airman Graham tagged along as well. He was a wiry guy – smart – although he struck Jack as being perpetually anxious about something.

Burr pushed his way through the heavy plywood and metal door and walked out of the building into the desert night. There was nothing in front of them but a barbed wire fence about a hundred meters off. Beyond that, it was all desert. Although it was dark out, it was still extremely hot and the absolute lack of any kind of breeze made the air suffocating. A large wooden flight of stairs ascending up the back of the operations building allowed access to its flat sandstone roof. Burr scaled the stairs quickly and motioned for Graham and Jack to follow. Once at the top, Jack looked around to an incredible perspective of the night-time surrounding area. Burr pointed out several landmarks including the rest of the base and airstrip, which was well-lit behind them. About a mile to the north was the Tigris River and to the east was a large city about two miles away. Lights flickered in the distance to indicate that the city he spoke of was real, but they couldn't see the river in the dark. More faraway lights flashing just above the horizon indicated the return of an Army helicopter patrol, which according to Burr, was a common sight. They were conducting their air-to-ground strafing runs just outside of the base perimeter, something that was known to Burr and the rest of the airmen simply as "the wire."

Jack asked Burr what he knew about the building that they were standing on. "Well, folks say it was some sort of command-and-control building when the Iraqis were here," he said. "Apparently, there was a big stand-off when the Army came through in 2003 and that's where all of the bullet holes came from," referencing the pockmarks that had caught Jack's eye earlier. "Supposedly, this whole base was the site of an Iraqi military academy during Saddam's regime and he flew in here all the time."

Standing on top of a captured enemy building that had been visited by Saddam Hussein felt momentarily unnerving to Jack. It was one thing to read about the atrocities of Iraq's former dictator and to consider the fratricidal brutality that his regime had represented, but to stand here among some of the actual relics of that not-at-all distant era made the existence of those evils seem more real. Equally unnerving was the way Airman Burr had casually taken them up to the roof of this building – without body armor and helmets. From here, Jack could see aircraft conducting actual combat operations. He felt exposed up there and he wanted to low-crawl back to the ladder and take cover. To Burr there was no big deal. "Just give it a few weeks," he said. "You'll get used to it."

Back inside the command post, Burr checked the flight schedule and reported that a C-130, a large cargo plane, was due in any time. He passed Jack a hand set that was connected to one of the battered green radios that sat in the corner of the room by a twisted and fraying cord. The radio itself was covered in many years' worth of dust and Jack thought it looked archaic enough to be a leftover from the jungles of Vietnam. Within minutes, the muffled squawking of the C-130's radio call broke the otherwise silent airwaves. "Flyfish Charlie Papa, Flyfish Charlie Papa this is Gold 19." Burr translated the call as an initial contact from the crew. "Flyfish Charlie Papa" was the call sign Jack would answer to. Flyfish was for FOB Sherman while Charlie Papa represented the phonetic alphabet's initials for Command Post. Jack pushed the transmitter and replied, conjuring up his most official-sounding voice.

"Gold 19, Gold 19, this is Flyfish Charlie Papa, go ahead."

"Copy that, we are fifteen mikes out, expecting MEDEVAC upload, how copy?"

Jack heard them loud and clear, but looked at Burr with urgency to see what he should do next. Burr instructed Jack to acknowledge the radio call, and then call the Army clinic to find out how many patients they were sending out on this particular bird. Jack picked up a phone and called the clinic, the number of which had been scrawled on a sticky note and slapped to the bottom of one of the computer monitors. This was the first act that Jack would legitimately perform in wartime operations – a telephone call coordinating the evacuation of troops that had just been injured in the field – and the incongruity of the sticky note made Jack pause.

A Private First Class answered the phone at the clinic.

"How many casualties do you have going out on Gold 19?" Jack asked quickly.

"Two on litters, one ambulatory." The PFC hung up just as quickly. No chit-chat.

Jack looked at Burr again. The older airman didn't hesitate.

"Call the aircrew. Now."

Jack passed them the information and then called the load crews over their intercom to let them know that a plane was due in about fifteen minutes. They would be responsible for marshaling the plane into its parking space and handling manifests and any necessary transfer of cargo. Three ramp workers scampered out of the break room, out of the door and took off to receive the plane. Burr looked at Jack and nodded with approval. "Good job," he said. "You got your first radio call under your belt. That's eighty percent of the job here, really." Jack smiled and felt a rush of satisfaction that helped keep his drowsy eyes open for the rest of the night.

By dawn, they'd run two more missions and Jack was operating purely on adrenaline. Burr had left at about 0500 hours to pack his gear before he departed later in the day. It had been about twenty hours since Jack had risen from his bunk in Qatar the previous day. At about 0700 hours, the familiar faces of Sergeants Hartman and Davidson appeared in the doorway, freshly rested since they'd parted ways last night. "What's up, buddy?" asked Blake. "Hartman here'll relieve ya for the day. Let's go get your CHU set up." Jack's sleep-deprived brain took a moment to translate "CHU" into "Containerized Housing Unit," which proved to be a glorified shipping pod with a door cut into it. Like every object, regulation, and structure in the military, CHUs had an official name, as well as a name the actual users bestowed. Blake and Jack hopped into the same white Dodge pickup they'd ridden from the flight line and jostled off over the pavement and back onto the taxiway.

In the early morning light, Jack could see with much greater clarity that the command post was not the only tenant of this airfield. Directly next to their building was a pole barn-type structure that Blake pointed out as the airfield fire department. Blake adopted a deep, radio-announcer voice, identifying buildings with increasing faux pomposity as they sped across the pavement. Up ahead was the Army aviation unit. Four Apache helicopters sat outside an enormous fabric hanger that had been erected to provide shelter for these flying gun platforms. These belonged to the guys Jack had seen in action from the roof the night before.

Instead of turning left onto the flight line, Blake took a hard right, which led them past some abandoned Iraqi bunkers and a guarded checkpoint. Two African men with thick accents commanded them to stop and produce identification. Armed to the teeth, these men were dressed not in the digital camouflage pattern of the US military, but in solid tan fatigues. Davidson leaned over and whispered to Jack that they were Ugandans. He handed one of them his ID card and flashed a smile. The guard's eyes lit up. "Ahh, Mee-stah Blake." he said, as if announcing Blake's presence to his colleague. Then his eyes sharpened in Jack's direction. "And who's *theese*, Mee-stah Blake?" Blake said that Jack was a new guy and that he was ok. "Let me see his card," replied the Ugandan, raising his eyebrows and simultaneously narrowing his eyes, which is not an easy thing to accomplish. Jack handed his identification over and the guard looked at both the front and back of it with great care. "Ok," he concluded. "You may go." He waved them on as Blake gunned the engine and rolled past the small plywood guard shack that stood by the road. "Mercenaries," he said, looking at Jack as he drove. "The government brings them over from Africa to handle security because they're tough and cheap. Great combo for a security guard, right?" He smiled. "They're really crazy." Jack didn't doubt him a bit.

As they tore down the badly decaying road, new scenery appeared all around them. On their left they passed a billboard-like wall that had once borne a tribute to Saddam Hussein in the form of an enormous mural of his mustachioed face. They could still make out most of it, except for where pieces of his face had been chipped off in a gesture of defiance. Ahead of them was another sandstone building, distinguished by its tower which sprouted radio antennas like a metallic garden on its roof. There was no mistaking that place as anything other than an air traffic control tower. As they drove closer Jack could see that it too was covered with the same type of pock marks that scarred the command post.

They'd gone about a half mile past the checkpoint when Blake turned off the road towards a walled-off area where their CHUs were. He had stopped using the radio-announcer voice. The blast walls that obscured them from view had obviously been placed there to protect the housing arrangements from any mortars or shell fragments that might find their way into the vicinity. Blake stopped the truck and they both got out and walked through an opening in the concrete. Behind the barrier was a metallic sub-division of about thirty-five CHUS, all aligned in neat rows and strung together with a single electrical cable that Jack presumed provided power for a light source. He and Blake walked over to one in the third row as Blake pulled a set of keys out of his pocket. "Garrison gave these to me last night," he said, fumbling with them between his fingers. "Here we go. CHU number sixty-four." Still carrying his body armor and gear, Jack pushed open the door and noticed the shining brass door handle that looked way out of place on this CHU that looked more like a dumpster than an actual building. It said something in Arabic just under the keyhole and he wondered what it meant.

Inside the CHU, the furnishings were Spartan to say the least. Two beds were on each end of the interior, and two large lockers in which to store gear. A single fluorescent light bulb poked out of the ceiling to light the place. Thankfully, the CHUs were air conditioned and provided some relief from the desert heat that was rising into the hundreds outside. Jack threw his bags down as Blake left him alone to settle in. "Be outside at eleven o'clock," he said. "The bus will be by around then to pick you up for work." Jack nodded although he had no idea what kind of transportation service he was referring to or even what time it was now. He looked down at his watch and saw that it was just after 0700 hours - only four hours till he had to be up again. He unpacked a few essential items from his bags, spread his grey wool blanket over the bare mattress and promptly fell asleep.

3

David Holman's alarm clock had gone off too soon and announced the start of his first full day on the job. As he rubbed the sleep out of his eyes, it took him a second to remember where he was and what he was doing inside of an oversized tin box. His mind raced as it tried to catch up with his surroundings. On the other side of the CHU was a second bed. On it he saw a few blankets and other personal items that indicated that he had a roommate, something he hadn't even noticed when he had arrived the night before. He thought of Kristine and wondered what she might be doing at this moment. "Would she be asleep now?" he thought. The eight-hour time difference was more than David's mind cared to compute this soon after waking. He sighed as the weight of having just begun this marathon bore down on his psyche. "What have I gotten myself into?" he thought, blearily.

David had thirty minutes to get ready before he caught the bus that Blake had told him about the night before, so he got dressed as quickly as possible to make sure he was on time. Then he headed out the door to utilize the bathroom facilities – located in a trailer that seemed like the focal point of this particular CHU compound. David opened the door and looked around inside. "Exactly like Afghanistan," he thought to himself. There were three stalls along the back wall as well as two showers opposed by four sinks and a large mirror that ran the length of the trailer. Everything was white. The only thing that wasn't up to typical standards was the tap water. It was strictly non-potable, so David helped himself to a liter of bottled water from a pallet that had been parked just outside the bathroom door. He brushed his teeth with that. Of course, it was beyond warm, having set for untold hours in the sun's furnace-like heat.

David showered, shaved and headed back to his CHU. He glanced at his watch. It was about five minutes before eleven which meant he had just enough time to gather his things and catch the bus. He strapped on his 9mm leg holster and made sure the magazine clip was loaded securely.

In Afghanistan, David had hated the idea of carrying a weapon. "If it comes down to us having to use these things, we're already screwed," he had said repeatedly. He had always been uncomfortable with firearms and despite the military's training, the extra responsibility of carrying a loaded one still made him instinctively nervous. It had been a while since David had worn a side arm and now, that feeling of extra weight at his hip made him walk with unnatural self-conscience as the door of his CHU closed behind him.

The concrete wall that surrounded the living compound opened up next to the road where the bus was supposed to stop. A couple of other airmen were standing near the entry-way and they turned around, squinting in the sun's heat as David approached. Jack Doolittle was among them and he smiled when he saw the familiar face of his traveling companion.

"Sergeant Holman," he announced playfully. "Long

time no see."

"It didn't seem that long to me," David replied, already wiping a bead of sweat from his forehead. The sun was hot and for the first time he was feeling the full force of Iraq's desert climate in late summer. He wondered how Jack was adjusting to the deployed conditions so far.

"How's your CHU?" he asked.

"Not too bad, not too bad. Practically the lap of luxury compared to what it could be." A smile creased Jack's face as he spoke. "How's yours?"

David laughed. "More like the *lack* of luxury."

Within minutes, a dust-covered bluebird bus that looked like it was within view of its last mile, sputtered and creaked to a halt in front of the waiting airmen. The glass panels of its narrow door folded away to reveal none other than Blake Davidson at the wheel. An AC/DC song blared from two speakers that had been duct-taped to the dashboard. "All right, guys, here're the newbies," he shouted. Jack stepped aboard and looked down the aisle at about fifteen airmen brandishing M16s. "This is Jack Doolittle, everybody. The other guy's name is Dave something. They just got in last night." David worked his way to an empty seat and wondered if Davidson ever slept. "We all ready?" Blake asked. Without waiting for a response, he hit the gas pedal. Dust filled the inside of the bus. "Next stop, chow hall." Dust was shaking loose from the ceiling of the bus like it was a salt shaker and some of the other passengers pulled bandanas and scarves over their noses and mouths to keep the particles out.

In the seat in front of Jack's was a relaxed dude wearing A1C stripes and a pair of goggles around his neck like Blake's that proved he was also part of the ramp crew. He turned around and calmly asked "What's up?" He took a sip of a freshly-opened energy drink, which was surely already filling with dust.

"Not much," Jack replied. He coughed into his shoulder. "Is it always this dusty?"

"Hans Drago," the relaxed gentleman said, offering a handshake. "And yeah, it's pretty much been like this since I got here."

Jack wasn't sure if the dude was telling him his name or speaking in tongues.

"I'm sorry, what was that first part?"

"Hans Drago," he repeated. "That's my name." Jack returned his handshake.

"Oh sure, mine's Jack. How long you been here?"

"'Bout three days. My unit came in on the same plane as Davidson up there. This looks like it will be a pretty crazy place, all the bullet holes and whatnot." Jack nodded and glanced out the window as they passed an army Humvee speeding down the road in the opposite direction. "Yeah," he said, "should be interesting."

Hans introduced Jack to some others from his outfit as the bus continued to spew dust all over them. Across the aisle was his supervisor, Technical Sergeant Carl Lee. He had a serious face and reeked of stale smoke. Behind him was a senior airman named Clark Wilson. Although he was about the same age as Lee, the lower-ranking Wilson seemed to imitate his boss's demeanor. Wilson's teeth were yellowed and crooked. Besides those two, Staff Sergeants Kathryn Jason and Kelly Shaw were also on the bus, as well as Airman Tony Graham, all of whom Jack had met the night before. He nodded in acknowledgement. In front of Hans sat another Senior Airman who looked as though he was twice Jack's age. Hans said that his name was Wayne Parsons and gave Jack a quick summary of his career. A prior Marine who had initially served in the late '70s, Parsons had apparently re-enlisted in the Air National Guard after 9/11 and had perpetually failed to make rank since then. Jack nodded and tried to make a mental note of the names Hans had been rattling off.

The introductions were cut off by the bus's arrival at the dining facility. Jack glanced around at the rest of the passengers, knowing he would probably meet them later. Blake stopped the bus in a roped–off section of gravel and pulled the lever to open the door. The passengers piled out and made their way towards the giant pole-barn with several wooden checkpoint areas constructed in front of it.

As Jack neared the checkpoints, he could see that they were manned by Ugandan guards in their tan uniforms, just like the ones who had stopped him and Blake the day before on the airfield. Each of the airmen was stopped as they filed past the barricade by a guard who asked to look at their ID cards and weapons. After ensuring that all weapons were on "safe," they were allowed entry into the chow hall.

Stepping inside of the chow hall was like stepping into another world. It wasn't a palace by stateside standards but compared to the CHUs and broken-down Iraqi leftovers that Jack had been inside so far, he almost felt like calling this place Buckingham. Rows upon rows of tables and chairs sat in front of two enormous buffet lines of food. Iraqi civilians had been hired to dish out the grub to the American troops. They darted back and forth, in and out of the kitchen, making sure there was enough food, slopping steaming hash browns and green beans onto the plates of each troop as they made their way down the line. Haggard Army grunts shuffled up to the dessert line and helped themselves to pieces of cake, as specially-designated Iraqi dealt ice cream sundaes to customers upon request. Above it all hung the individual flags of each one of the fifty states. It was a surreal thing to see, but Jack took it all in as he filled his plate heartily.

With a plateful of hash browns and an omelet, he sat down at one of the tables. Kathryn Jason sat down directly across from him and next to her was Kelly Shaw. They were two of only three females on the shift. In conversation with them, he found out that they had both been deployed several times in the past few years. As load planners, they would be working in the command post with him. Wayne Parsons interrupted and sat down on Jack's left. "Chow was a lot different back in the 'Corps, a lot different," he blurted. "All we ever got was K-rations, never any of this four-star stuff." He began digging away at a massive slice of cheesecake.

Jack smiled, but turned his attention elsewhere. It was hard to focus on anything in particular for very long in this place. All around them were the sights and sounds of men and women enjoying a temporary break from war. As an observer to it all, Jack noticed the weariness that was apparent on almost all of their faces. At the table in front of theirs sat a group of Rangers who looked like they'd just made it back from the field. Each one of them was bearded and covered from head to toe in pasty white desert dust. Their weapons were obviously used and some of their uniforms were torn. Despite their grizzled appearance, here they were, sipping on juice boxes and enjoying another can of yogurt before they went back to work. The juxtaposition of these sights was almost absurd. For these warriors, the chow hall was more than just a place to eat, it was a chance to escape the vicious reality of their deployed lives and experience a brief but therapeutic reminder of normalcy. Of course, for some of these soldiers, there was no way of knowing whether or not the meal they were enjoying would be their last. The realization of that vital utility made Jack appreciate the dining facility even more.

Above the chatter of voices at the table, the sound of Wayne's drawling still rang in Jack's ears. Now he was saying something about the Air Force being full of "wanna-bes." Jack shoveled his hash browns and got up from the table with everyone else. David Holman spoke to Jack as they walked out of the building. "What do you think so far?" he asked.

"Of what?"

"Deployment."

Jack's brain hadn't fully processed the idea yet. He looked down at his boots, then back at David. "I don't know, seems like a pretty wild place."

"Maybe," said David. "You'll get into the routine in a few days. The first month is always the hardest to get through, except maybe for the last month. At the beginning, you keep thinking about how much time you have left and at the end, you fixate on how little time you have left. At least that's how it is for me."

"Kind of like prison, huh?"

"A very dangerous prison, maybe," David replied. He wasn't smiling.

They headed in one gigantic gaggle back through the Ugandans' checkpoint, around a maze of concrete blast walls and out into the blistering heat to climb aboard the bus once again.

Jack pulled his wide-brimmed boonie hat low over his eyes to block out the sun. He didn't look up when an army Major passed by, going the opposite direction.

Clark Wilson turned and spat towards Jack, seeing that he hadn't rendered the customary salute. "Don't worry; this place is a no-salute zone."

"Oh, I hadn't even thought about that," replied Jack.

They all got back on the bus and Doolittle sat down next to Hans again as Blake fired up the engine and guided the wheel to avoid the dozens of Humvees and M-RAP personnel carriers that were parked outside of the dining facility. With food resting in their bellies, everyone was pretty quiet the rest of the way to the Command Post, except for Blake, who was singing along to the music piping through the feeble dashboard speakers.

When they pulled in to the yard of the Command Post, Jack finally got a good look at it in daylight. The building looked even more rickety than it had the night before and the American flag was still hanging limp on the duct-taped flagpole. Pallets of cargo waiting to be shipped out sat haphazardly around the yard and a couple of forklifts could be seen parked under an awning adjacent to the main structure. Blake let everyone off the bus in front of the building and they filed past the painted eagle that Jack had noticed the night before. Captain Garrison was standing in the doorway of his office, looking at a map on the wall and he smiled as they walked in and separated off to their work areas. Jack walked into the radio room and saw Sergeant Hartman diligently working at his computer while another Senior Airman sat by the radios in the chair that Jack had occupied the night before. Three load planners sat on the other side of the room and were promptly replaced by Graham, Jason and Shaw.

Sergeant Hartman looked up from the computer monitor as David walked into the room and asked how he liked his CHU. "It's ok," said David, "Although I didn't have a lot of time in it." Hartman motioned towards the guy who was sitting in Jack's seat.

"Well, this is your roommate, Holman – Senior Airman Tyndall. He's the controller who'll be working dayshifts. I figure keeping you on nights as shift supervisor is the way to go." David nodded his head in acknowledgement. Tyndall looked up, but said nothing as he collected up his gear and walked out. His brusque manner puzzled David. He looked at Sergeant Hartman. "Is he ok?"

"I guess so. He just has his own way of doing things."

David shrugged. "To each his own, I guess."

Jack took over the desk that Tyndall had vacated and glanced at the flying schedule for the day. Three missions for the afternoon and evening. He looked forward to the easy pace that would help him get the hang of things. Hartman collected his gear and checked out for the day. "Have a good shift," he said. "Hope it's not too crazy."

They ran the three missions, all C-130s with routine cargo loads, and for each one of them Jack made the radio calls and notifications exactly as Airman Burr had explained the night before. Burr was already gone, having departed that morning, but Jack was confident that Burr would have complimented him on his performance if he had been there. For David, deployed command post operations were a familiar routine and the experience he'd gained in Afghanistan was coming back to him in a flood.

During the down time between flights, David explained the way the shifts would work to make sure Jack was aware of the schedule. He and Jack would come in with the rest of the night shift at 1300 hours, or 1 o'clock in the afternoon. Tyndall and Hartman would relieve them at one in the morning and work their twelve hours while

Jack and David slept back at the housing compound. That way, there would always be a controller on duty and they would each have their CHUs to themselves while not at work.

David assured Jack that while things may have seemed slow just then, the intensity could rise at any moment. With no days off, the pace would be fairly grueling. As Holman laid out the situation, Jack reminded himself again that in this war they had it easy compared to troops in the field. Many others had it a lot worse off than they did.

Outside, the sun was gone and things started to cool off a bit in the darkness. Hartman and Tyndall were back at 0100 hours to relieve Jack and David, along with the rest of the day shift. They piled back into the old bus and rode back to the CHU compound with Blake at the wheel.

Jack walked back to his CHU and opened the door, anxious to get back to sleep. He fumbled through his personal bag for a moment and pulled out a tiny calendar. Opening the pages to the month of September, he drew a line through the date and looked at it with satisfaction. One down, one hundred and eighty-two to go.

4

The first few weeks at FOB Sherman passed quickly for Jack Doolittle. The routine of daily life was something to which he quickly adapted, though before long, he began to feel as if an invisible cast-iron field was locking him, day after day, into the same monotonous sequence of events. Get up – shave – catch the bus. Chow – work – catch the bus. Shower – bed – repeat. Not that the routine was bad; living the same day over and over again was getting easy. As a newcomer to this kind of lifestyle, Jack was beginning to think that the whole deployment scheme was a pretty good way to make some easy money. Of course, there was the occasional tense moment while dealing with fatigued aircrews on the radio, but all in all, Iraq didn't seem nearly as bad as he had expected.

September twenty-eighth started out no differently than any other day had up to that point. Jack sat up in his bed and looked over at Tyndall's mess piled on the other side of their CHU. He got up, stumbled to the whitewashed bathroom trailer, shaved, and caught the bus with the others just as usual. They'd all been on shift at the Command Post for a couple of hours but were still waiting for their first mission of the day. Jack was sitting at his desk, quietly formatting the next day's flying schedule. Tony Graham sat at his computer on the other side of the room while the others were occupying their time as best as they could. David Holman had driven over to the PX with Wayne Parsons, Hans Drago crowded with some of the others around the TV in the break room. Jack looked over at Tony Graham and offered him some peanuts from his bag. "Thanks, are these from that care package you got the other day?"

Without warning, a siren began to blare at an incredible volume. A pre-recorded female voice echoed across the public address system; "ROCKET ATTACK, ROCKET ATTACK." Tony Graham's chair slid out from underneath him as he dove to take cover. Then a violent crack of thunder felt like it shook the entire earth right out from under them. This was like no kind of thunder Jack had ever heard before. Blake came bursting into the room from outside, hollering and gesturing wildly with his hands.

"You gotta see this, man!"

Meanwhile, the sirens were still blaring their horrendous shrieks. Blake's eyes were also blazing and there was a catch in his voice that told Jack that whatever Blake had just seen was something he might not want to see for himself after all. Jack could feel his throat tighten and he hesitated for a moment, but his curiosity shouted at him to get out of the seat and go. He jumped up from the desk and skidded down the hallway behind Blake. Together they crashed through the outer door of the building at almost the same time. Jack glanced up and spotted a plume of dust and smoke a little less than a quarter of a mile down the flight line from them. "Oh, my gosh," he muttered.

Not two seconds had passed before the biggest roaring sound he'd ever felt shook the earth again. Blake grabbed Jack's shoulder and they both ducked behind the closest concrete blast wall and then dived back indoors. Jack could taste the grit of dust in his mouth as he pressed himself as closely to the ground as possible. Then it was silent again, except for Jack's heart pounding wildly against the floor tiles.

He looked up at Blake, who was crouching just inside the doorway. The sergeant's face was murky from the dust that had stuck to his sweaty face during the commotion. His teeth cracked a wide and wicked smile as he nervously spat out a laugh.

"Are we crazy or what, man? We just got mortared!"

Jack twitched a smile too.

"Guess we earned our combat zone pay today, huh?"

As Jack got up and dusted himself off, the same mechanical voice came across the public address system: "ALL CLEAR, ALL CLEAR." As quickly as it had begun, the attack was over. "Is that it?" asked Jack. His eyes were darting around madly. Blake clasped the younger man on the shoulder. "Yep, all clear. You're a veteran now, buddy." Jack waved the sergeant off and returned to his desk in the command post. An eerie silence hung over the building as he went back to editing the flying schedule, just as he had been before the sirens went off. To Jack it felt as though no one else cared what had happened.

Captain Garrison finally checked in on things in the command post. "Are we all good?" he asked.

"I guess so. Are they always that close?"

Garrison took his glasses off and wiped the dust from the lenses with his shirt. "Those two were pretty close. Just be thankful the sirens went off this time."

"You mean they don't always work?"

"No, it's really hit or miss with the way these things

happen. There's supposed to be a sensor system that activates when a rocket or mortar passes over the base. It's pretty spotty, though, so by the time someone sees the incoming and activates the alarm, the attack is usually over already."

"You'd think they'd have something safer than that to get the word out."

'Well, luckily, the bad guys can't aim worth a darn."

Jack took no comfort in Garrison's words. Later that day he silently placed his body armor under his desk in the command post so it would be within reach if they ever had a closer call.

The eeriness of that day changed the way Jack perceived the entire deployment experience. He hadn't stared into the face of an enemy or even come remotely close to pulling a trigger in combat, but those two explosions finally made his presence in Iraq seem real. It bothered him that contrary to his training in boot camp, the alarms there seemed to have been arbitrary and unreliable.

The biggest impact that those first mortars had on Jack – and the rest of the Airmen working at the Command Post – was that they announced the presence of an enemy who was willing to go to extreme lengths to exterminate them. Like most of the opposition faced by American forces in Iraq, those responsible had been hired by al-Qaeda's emergent terror network in Iraq. They could easily have been kids, paid off by the powers-that-be to implement guerrilla warfare. There was no way for the troops at FOB Sherman to understand what would motivate violent opposition of this kind, but their preferred tactics were clear. Under the cover of night, they would easily sneak within range of the FOB and set up some old mortar equipment in the desert. A washing machine timer or even a block of ice cleverly attached to the barrel or firing mechanism could delay the weapon's discharge by hours, so that the culprit could safely escape the area. By the time the mortar was actually fired, the perpetrator would be miles away in safety when American forces were dispatched to investigate the area. The blast itself wouldn't be very accurate, but the unnerving spontaneity of the explosion would be enough to interrupt normal operations on the FOB.

As the days passed at FOB Sherman, Jack also became increasingly aware of the fact that the very ground they walked upon had once been trodden by Saddam Hussein and his subordinates merely half a decade earlier. The sandstone and rock that stared back at him as he walked to his CHU from the latrine every night had been the landscape on which some of history's most unthinkable violations of human rights had brutally unfolded. Jack often pondered the helplessness of those lost souls who were victimized by Saddam's terrorizing regime.

One particularly haunting reminder of the ghosts that inhabited this place was a soccer stadium that the bus passed on its daily trek to the chow hall. Though in total disrepair after being heavily bombed, it was said that Saddam had once executed an entire Olympic soccer team there for failing to rate a medal during the international games. Now, a once-majestic reviewing podium jutted out from the rest of the grandstand, looking very much like the jawbone of a cracked and battered skull. Two opposite wings of stadium seats extended from either side of the main structure, wrapping around the outer half of the unkempt field to form the arms of this shattered death skeleton. In front of it stood a series of multi-colored pillars which supported a gnarly sculpture of a coiled serpent. Under it all, inlayed tiles spelled out in Arabic the name *Al-Hayya,* or "The Snake".

Rumors of other local atrocities were rampant among the service members deployed at FOB Sherman. They encompassed everything from underground torture chambers to a program that Saddam reportedly commissioned at this airfield in the 1980s to construct remote-controlled drones that could spread anthrax like crop-dusters. Regardless of what actually happened at this place, it had indeed been crawling with Special Forces of the infamous Iraqi Republican Guard and all kinds of brass from the top echelons of the Ba'ath party. Murals of Saddam in eerily personable poses were still everywhere, from the sides of bombed-out buildings to the billboard-like tributes posted every so often like the one by the Ugandan's airfield guard shack. Abandoned bunkers were also plentiful and from most of their bullet-riddled appearances, it was not difficult to imagine Republican Guard officers making their last stand as the US Army overran the base during the shock-and-awe campaign that crushed Iraq's organized military in early 2003.

Once when Jack had some down time, he wandered inside of a bunker that had been dug adjacent to the airfield. It was no more than a concrete-reinforced hole in the ground from which a metal pipe had been run to the surface to provide some form of air circulation. Kicking around among the mildewed trash that covered the floor, Jack found a lone pair of Iraqi military boots, perfectly laced and ready for service. He picked up one of them and turned it over to examine the sole. Stamped clearly on the bottom was the red triangle insignia of the Republican Guard. A cold draft blew through the stuffy air of the glorified pit, which Jack thought unusual considering that the outdoor temperature was over a hundred degrees in the shade. He returned the boot to its place alongside its partner and crawled back into the daylight as quickly as he could.

As much as the ghosts of FOB Sherman's past permeated every stone on which the base was built, they seemed to haunt the local population even more. Iraqi civilians would gather in the shadows of Saddam's old soccer stadium a couple of days a week to sell trinkets and souvenirs to servicemen who were interested in taking home an authentic piece of Middle Eastern culture. The dealers themselves – screened and inspected along with their goods by Army MPs – were probably just as interested in catching a glimpse of American culture through their customers. The resulting interactions were capable of breaking and warming a heart at almost the same time.

On a slow afternoon, Blake Davidson, Wayne Parsons, David Holman and Jack Doolittle piled into one of the Dodge pickups and drove over to the bazaar to check out the merchandise. The locals had set up a number of tents at what was once the inner field of the abandoned soccer stadium. They peddled their wares on low-standing tables that were overflowing with rugs, scarves, elaborate knives and a myriad of other exotic relics. As they pulled up to the makeshift market, Jack was surprised to see that the Iraqis there were not the black-robed, bearded Arabs he had expected to see. Much to the contrary, they looked westernized and professional in blue jeans, sports jerseys and polo shirts. The airmen got out of the truck and walked up to the tents. An attractive girl, probably in her late teens, emerged from behind one of the tables and offered them fresh tea in a vocabulary of perfectly-accented English. All four of the Americans accepted and watched for a minute or two as she served each of them the steaming-hot beverage in elegant cups of china. The tea itself, which the girl referred to as *chai,* was richly flavored but not nearly as sweet as Jack had expected it to be. It packed a mighty punch of caffeine.

The girl's father soon appeared and courteously suggested that the Americans look over his merchandise that was proudly displayed on a couple of tables. He was balding and sported a thick black mustache. He tried to make small talk by asking where each was from. "Michigan," David replied. Instantly the Iraqi's eyes lit up. "Ah, yes," he said, tilting his head back with surprise. "Dearborn is in Michigan. My brother-in-law lives there. Do you know him?" David Holman laughed and admitted that he did not know the man's kin. The Iraqi merchant laughed anyway and once again encouraged the Americans to inspect his tables of goods. David obliged and examined the wares, most of which were cheap knickknacks, knock-off watches and jewelry. David felt a little guilty for not buying anything after being offered such hospitality, so he plunked down a couple of bucks for a carved camel figurine, which the man gratefully accepted. David moved on to the other tables.

The next booth was obviously that of a specialized rug dealer who turned out to be a guy about Jack Doolittle's age. His name was Mahmood. He was tall and lean with a crop of coal-black scruff on his face. His eyes were wide and open, the whites seeming exaggerated by their contrast to his dark complexion. One of the smaller rugs on his table caught Jack's eye and he asked the Iraqi how much he wanted for it. "Fifty," was the answer he gave. Again, Jack was surprised at the man's knowledge of English. They haggled over the price a bit, Jack feeling he was on the set of an old movie, and finally agreed on forty. As Jack picked the rug up and placed it under his arm, he asked the Iraqi how often he came to the bazaar here.

"Every week for three years," he said. "I live in town. Selling is my only income. My father was killed by the Iraqi military. He worked for the US Marines as an informant. He did not like Saddam. Then my mother died soon afterward. I think her heart was broken." Sobered, Jack nodded his head in acknowledgement; though he knew there was no way to fully understand this world in which Mahmood lived.

Jack looked around at the other dealers who stood in various poses around the bazaar, trying desperately to sell their merchandise to Davidson, Parsons, and Holman. He wondered about the horrors that they must have seen in the decades of turmoil that had afflicted their homeland. Not knowing at all what to say, Jack thanked Mahmood for the rug and asked the others if they were ready to go. Mahmood grasped Jack's hand and said, "Please come back," with a look of sincerity in his eye. The four Americans piled back into their Dodge and drove back to the command post in silence.

5

October and November came and went at FOB Sherman and David Holman found himself counting down the days until he reached the half-way point of his tour. The mental challenge of this deployment was beyond anything he had anticipated when he'd volunteered to come to this place. He often thought back to his time in Afghanistan and the gung-ho enthusiasm he had felt while he was there. "Was it really that way?" he asked himself daily, remembering. Now he felt as though he was growing older by the day and he could see proof of it in the mirror. Just that morning he had noticed new strands of gray appearing along his hairline.

He missed Kristine desperately. He'd left her to pursue this deployment six months into their married life and now he felt guilty when he considered the decision he had made. "She could resent this so easily," but she didn't, and she reassured him of that fact in almost every letter that he received from her. He had gotten another from her today. Opening the envelope slowly, David imagined Kristine addressing it to him at their dining room table at home. It put a smile on his face at first, but as he read her outpouring of love on the page, David was overcome by the realization of how distant he now felt from her.

That night, he tried to tell her some of the things he

had been thinking about in his own letter. "This time of separation isn't a bad thing," he wrote. "I thought that by coming here, I'd experience the same sense of purpose that I felt while I was deployed before. I now realize that my purpose is at home, with you." He looked at the page he'd written and scowled. The words seemed so empty and contrived. Was there nothing he could do to make her feel just a little closer? He folded the paper in half and shoved it in its envelope to mail the next morning.

    David tried to sleep, but it did not come easily. He'd usually toss and turn before nodding off, only to wake again in a few hours. The pattern was becoming a part of the routine of life that David dreaded. He would sometimes stare at his travel alarm clock, watching the minutes tick by until it was time to rise for the day. His mind was definitely unsettled by the anticipation of a rocket attack and the continual racket of aircraft engines and machine gun fire, but most of all, his restlessness was due to the distance between him and Kristine. The time difference meant that she would be at work during the hours he was trying to sleep and his mind raced at the thought of what she might be doing at the office while he was lying there, staring at the digits on his alarm clock. He was so tired. But he had to get up for work.

    The moderate pace of operations that they had arrived into was gone and it seemed that while on duty, David was constantly bellowing parking assignments and cargo information into the speaker of his radio equipment. In turn, the ramp crews seemed to spend their entire days on the flight line, zigzagging around in forklifts loaded with pallets of cargo expressed to the US Army. In addition to the standard C-130 and C-17 airframes used by the Air Force, they saw an increasing amount of activity from the

Iraqi Air Force's fleet. The fledgling military's air branch had obtained three antiquated C-130 "E" model planes that served as the backbone of their airlift corps. Their pilots were very green and David grew to expect long delays when dealing with them. But they were dedicated and served their country with pride. As the American ramp crews downloaded their cargo, the Iraqi aviators would usually disembark their aircraft and spread rugs over the concrete tarmac. Facing east, they would conduct the prayerful rituals of their faith before climbing back aboard and taking off for their next destination.

The international flavor of operations at FOB Sherman did not stop there. In order to relieve a fraction of the heavy workload that had been placed upon the aircrews of Air Force cargo planes, the Department of Defense had sought out contract agreements with civilian freight carriers from Europe and the Middle East. These companies sold the services of their Russian military surplus planes at lofty rates, but completed their missions dependably. Like their aircraft, many of the pilots who flew under their contracts were Russian veterans of the Cold War.

The planes themselves looked like flying junkyards. Typically, they were either Anotov AN-12's or Ilyushin IL-76's. Both models had been in use since at least the 1960s and these airframes that had now found their way into the skies of Iraq showed their wear. Hans Drago joked after watching an AN-12 spew oil as it took off from the airfield that it looked like it could drop out of the sky at any moment.

Hans's prediction was realized when another AN-12 skidded off the end of the runway a few weeks later. The pilot came in too hot on his landing approach and knocked out about eight of the lights that marked the end of the concrete strip. Although Jack Doolittle didn't see the actual crash, he knew something was awry when the radios went wild with excited cries from the ramp crew.

The two that yelled the loudest were Carl Lee and Blake Davidson. Carl shouted for everyone to stay back from the scene as Blake cursed loudly. After a couple of minutes passed, Carl called Jack specifically and asked that he come out to the plane to see if any official accident reports would be required. Captain Garrison joined him and they rode out to the end of the runway together in one of the dodge pickups.

An Army safety officer had already beaten them to the spectacle. Lee was there, too, representing the ramp team. He and the Army officer were staring in disbelief at the foreign aviator. Apparently, the pilot had just climbed from the cockpit when Garrison and Doolittle arrived. He was probably in his late fifties, an overweight man who was dressed for action in a bathrobe and a pair of flip-flops. He looked at the Americans innocently and raised his hands in the air as if he were holding forth his point of view so that they could all get a better look.

"What problem?" he asked, his English poor. "I land!"

He motioned towards the cockpit, apparently meaning to indicate that he had a great deal of experience at the controls. Jack noticed that there was a hula girl doll hanging in one of the side windows, as if the pilot was a teenager with a beater pick-up truck. Luckily, the Russian's skid off the end of the runway did little damage to his aircraft and his three crewmembers did not even appear to be shaken. The Russian took off again about an hour later with merely a bruised ego.

Weeks later, another AN-12 tried to land at FOB

Sherman's airfield in the midst of a horrific dust storm. By then, Jack had experienced a few of these ordeals that would envelope the desert like a Biblical plague and literally block out the sun for days at a time. The entire atmosphere seemed to turn rust-like and the particles of dust had clung to Jack's clothes, hair and even his eyelashes each time he had dared to venture into the oblivion.

The first time Jack experienced a true dust storm was on what began as a perfectly clear day, with a temperature in the lower hundreds. He happened to be sitting on the roof of the command post with Hans Drago and Blake Davidson during a lull in the afternoon's work. On the horizon, Hans spotted what looked like an ominously expanding rain cloud. "Looks like it's going to rain," he said. Jack was intrigued and got up to examine it. Hans was right behind him.

As the cloud approached, they could soon see that it was not a rain cloud at all, but a full-fledged dust barrage that was racing across the desert. The sandy fangs of this monster were closing in on them and the three flew down the creaking staircase to take refuge inside the building. Though tentatively safe from the storm, Jack's curiosity again got the best of him and he rushed to the door at the other side of the building to watch the cloud swallow them all up.

When it hit, the sky instantly turned a rusty red. The wind hit Jack's face and showered him with ashy debris as if he had been in the way of a massive explosion. He couldn't see or feel a thing, so he turned his head back inside the building and expected to breathe pure air into his deprived lungs, except there was none. Jack strained to see through the clouds of red soot that were forming in the hallways of the command post. Despite his rapidly shrinking field of vision due to the particles that were caking up around his eyelids, he could easily make out the streams of dust and wind that were pouring through each one of the individual bullet holes poked through the battered walls. It reminded him of the way water rushed into the hull of a mortally leaking ship.

Jack resolved to find a place to sit so at least he wouldn't bump into anything. He fumbled his way toward his desk of radios and nearly tripped over Wayne Parsons, who himself was staggering through the dust trying to take pictures of the mayhem with a digital camera. He had a bandana tied around his mouth to help block out some of the dust. Looking around the room, Jack could only make out a few silhouettes of human form. One face he could recognize was that of David Holman, whose white teeth gave his identity away as he calmly sat, smiling at the madness that was unfolding before him.

Jack found a chair and sat in it. The dust had spread thickly throughout the entire building by now and he could hear nothing but the howling of the outdoor wind as it rushed into the multitude of bullet holes and swirled its way into the mouths and lungs of each airman inside. Soon, the coughing of twenty-three Americans had swelled to a decibel that drowned out even the strongest gust. Sitting next to Jack was the silhouette of a man he could barely identify as Hans Drago. Hans leaned over to Jack and with a raspy voice asked, "Water please?"

Such was the environment that the Russian AN-12 tried to land in during a similar dust barrage. When these dust storms hit, flying operations would cease for several days at a time and those on the ground would usually lay low until the plague passed over. It was a good thing Jack happened to be sitting by the radios when the Russian pilot's voice broke through the airwaves. "Sherman Command Post, AN-12 Alpha-Golf-Alpha 1345, fifteen minutes out and beginning land pattern." Jack couldn't believe his ears. The airfield was obviously closed and the official weather status generously marked the range of visibility at less than two hundred meters. To safely land an AN-12, they needed to have at least eight hundred meters of clear sight. This guy was crazy. Jack radioed back to him.

"Alpha Gulf Alpha 1345, this is Sherman Command Post, be advised, airfield is closed due to poor visibility."

"No problem," was the reply. "I am best pilot. 200 meters, no problem."

"No, no, no," said Jack. "This airfield is closed."

There was a long pause on the other end of the horn. Finally, Jack talked him into a holding pattern to wait for things to clear up, which he knew wasn't going to happen any time soon. After about twenty minutes, the Russian called back.

"Beginning approach."

"No. This airfield is CLOSED."

The Russians finally complied and diverted to another airfield. The pilot was a guy that Jack had seen on the airfield before. He would fly in with a load of cargo about once a week and the ramp crew was familiar with his antics on the flight line. He was an uptight, wiry man with a thin and finely-groomed moustache that made him look like an aviator out of an old World War I movie.

About a month after the dust storm episode, he was due to come in again but never showed up. David Holman was on shift at that time, and he waited about two hours past the Russian's scheduled arrival time before he called the contractor's operations office in Dubai. A Middle Eastern woman's voice answered. Holman explained that the aircraft was late on arrival, and that he was wondering if he could still expect him in that day. "Oh, I'm sorry," said the cheery female voice. "That plane crashed just after departing Fallujah while in-route to your location. All seven crewmembers were killed. Do not expect the aircraft today, thank you." Click.

Her nonchalant and abrupt manner took Holman by surprise. Although there was only a dial tone at the other end of the line, he felt he should at least say something. Instead, he hung up the phone. Sometimes there just aren't any words to say.

6

If the flight line wasn't busy at night, Jack liked to sit on the roof of the command post. The sandstone blocks would always feel cool and from that vantage point he could watch the smattering of lights that peacefully flicked in the distance, off-base. There was a picnic table on the roof and Jack would often sip a cool soda and enjoy the quiet. He would sometimes think back to his arrival at FOB Sherman and his fear of going up to the roof with Tony Graham that first night. Now, being up here was one the few things he felt like he might miss when all this was a memory.

Jack heard steps coming from his left and turned to see David Holman climbing the ladder to join him on the roof. He sat down at the picnic table and took a deep breath. His eyes scanned the desert that lay below them and he took another deep breath.

"What's up, Jack?"

"Nothing much. Just sitting."

"Well, mind if I join you?" Jack nodded his approval.

David laughed. "Of course, I ask now that I'm already here." Jack shrugged, not feeling like chit-chat.

"You know this really sucks, being here," David said.

Jack looked at the older man, noting the fatigue that hung around his eyes like cobwebs.

"Do you ever sleep?"

David didn't say anything, but the expression on his face told Jack that the answer was no.

"Well, I really don't think it's that bad. I mean, it could be a lot worse. We could be out there someplace." Jack motioned with his hand beyond the base perimeter.

"Yeah, but I used to crave the excitement of all this, you know. Now, it's just not the same. I miss my wife. Maybe you wouldn't understand."

Jack nodded again, but had no idea what to say. Holman's sudden confessional had really caught him off guard.

"I can't imagine being married, man. Not at this point."

"Yeah," said David. "I used to feel that way, too." When I was in Afghanistan, I had this, I don't know, this angry passion about being over here. Now, I just don't know why I would have ever wanted to get back into a place like this."

"Yeah, I guess it's not easy."

"You know what's funny, though? On my first deployment, I never remember feeling scared or endangered. Here, I worry all the time. Do you realize that we could both be killed right here by a sniper or something?"

The thought hadn't occurred to Jack. He had just been enjoying the relative feeling of security on the roof.

"I just don't know what I'm doing here," concluded David.

There was a long pause and it made Jack even more uncomfortable. If Holman wanted to talk, he wasn't going to make him stop, though. He tried to change the subject to something lighter. "How long have you been married?"

he asked.

"Not very long."

"Hmm."

Another pause.

"Yeah, I don't know. I guess we'll all get through this," said David.

The two men were silent again. The lights of an Army helicopter flashed in the distance as they stared at what was in front of them. For a second, David felt as though he might have made a mistake opening up to Jack like this.

"I'm sorry, man. I didn't mean to get all weird on you."

"No, no, that's ok," said Jack. "I don't mind."

"Well, I think everyone has their own stuff that they carry around over here. It just gets to a point where it starts to wear on you, is all."

Jack nodded again and took a sip of his coke. He couldn't decide if he admired David for his openness or thought he was a bit of a sap. Then, abruptly, he got up and excused himself from the picnic table.

"Well, I'd better go. Gotta make sure somebody's watching the radios."

"No problem, man. Go ahead."

As he climbed back down the ladder, Jack felt a little surprised by the way he had left David up on the rooftop alone like that. "He'll be fine," he told himself.

That night, Jack was in his CHU getting ready for lights-out when the rocket alarms sounded again. Though Jack instinctively crouched to the floor for cover, a tic of excitement surged through his body. He heard several explosions nearby and decided that he would be safer in a concrete bunker than in his CHU. He darted out the door and ran for the closest shelter, located directly behind the bathroom trailer. As he traipsed across the gravel walkway, more explosions could be heard near the flight line. He ducked inside the bunker and was glad to see the familiar face of Wayne Parsons inside.

"This is nothing compared to Grenada," Parsons said, looking up at Jack, repeating a by now familiar yet endearing boast.

Jack looked at the older man with disbelief. "It's something, though!"

He leaned against the concrete wall and closed his eyes, relishing the surge of adrenaline as he caught his breath. Minutes later, the public address system blared once again. "ALL CLEAR, ALL CLEAR."

Wayne Parsons looked at Jack. "This concludes the evening's entertainment," he said. "I'm going back to my CHU."

Jack nodded in agreement and returned to his quarters. As he prepared for bed, he thought about what David had said earlier that night. "When you start to think about stuff like that; that's when you have a problem." Jack wasn't concerned a bit. "This is exciting stuff," he told himself. "Enjoy it while you're here."

7

Just before Christmas, a series of local elections would take place to determine Iraq's provincial leadership. It was obvious that this vote represented a milestone in Iraq's turmoil-laden path to democracy and the opponents to the country's new system of self-governance were bent on doing anything in their power to deter voters from the polls.

For a couple of weeks leading up the elections, Jack Doolittle noticed a new intensity in insurgent operations. It had become a morbid routine to climb onto the Command Post's roof at night. It wasn't silent anymore. Now he could watch the Army's Apache helicopters make their air-to-ground strafing runs outside of the base's perimeter with blazing intensity. As usual, Jack would climb the rickety ladder when the radios were silent, usually to find most of the ramp crew sitting on the sandstone walls, puffing on cigars. They'd cheer as if they were watching a Super Bowl touchdown when the helicopters spat their fifty-caliber rounds onto the enemy. Sometimes there would be an explosion, followed by even more cheers. Then, once the helicopters were through, there was silence again, but it wasn't the same kind of silence that had drawn Jack up to the roof before. This silence was eerie and brutal.

There was a tension in the air that everyone could

feel. It was as if they were all bracing themselves for something "big" to happen, but didn't dare speak of it with one another. Jack Doolittle felt as if sitting in the command post all day was becoming more and more like sitting in a pressure cooker.

"Nothing's happening," he said to David Holman one afternoon. "I wish something would just *happen*. We all know stuff is going on outside the wire. I wish something would just happen so we could do some real work for a change."

"Be careful what you wish for. I, for one, would take being bored over *something* happening any day. Besides, there's stuff going on right now; we've got a bunch of planes to track this afternoon."

"Yeah, but you know what I mean," said Jack.

"We're all stressed out here, man. Maybe you should try working out more often to blow off some steam."

Blake Davidson popped his head into the room. "Did I hear someone mention working out?"

"Yeah, I was just telling Jack that we should take advantage of the gym more often. I know I need it, too."

"Well, what are you waitin' for?" said Blake. "Gym tonight after work. Be there."

Minutes later, the phone rang. Jack answered.

"Command post, Airman Doolittle."

"Hi, this is Major Armstrong from the Army clinic. We've got a big load of Medevac patients going out this afternoon and were wondering if any of you would be able to lend a hand."

"Stand by, let me check on that," said Jack. He turned to David and explained the situation.

"Sure, go ahead if you want to. I'll stay back and watch the phones."

Jack turned his attention back to the voice on the other end of the line.

"Absolutely, sir. What time do I need to be there?"

"As soon as possible."

"Copy that."

Jack hung up the phone. "Well, I guess I'm going over to the clinic," he said to David.

"Ok, see ya later."

Jack left the command post and climbed into one of the Dodge pickups parked outside for general use. He'd never been to the Army clinic before, but he had a pretty good idea of how to get there from all the base maps he'd studied. Within minutes, he was climbing out of the truck and heading into the entrance of a solid brick building. It looked nothing like the rest of the structures Jack had seen on FOB Sherman. Instead of the decrepit sandstone that everything else was made of, the clinic appeared to have been built much more recently. He passed a sign on his left with a red cross on it, so he knew he was in the right place.

Inside, Jack walked up to a service counter and explained to an army specialist behind the desk why he was there.

"Follow that hallway, turn left and go out the back door," she said.

Jack followed the instructions and headed down the sterile corridor. On either side of him were wards occupied by wounded troops. He was walking quickly, but he could make out some of their faces as he passed. A man was slouched in a wheelchair near one of the doorways. His head was bandaged with blue gauze. "How ya doin'?" asked Jack as he walked by. There was no verbal answer, but the man's quizzical stare made Jack realize that his choice of words had been callous and poorly chosen. Clearly, the man was not well at all.

Jack continued down the hall and was soon outside again. He was greeted by Major Armstrong, with whom he had spoken on the phone.

"Thanks for volunteering," he said.

"Glad to help."

"If you could just stand over here with the others for now, the patients will be ready shortly." The Major pointed towards an ambulance parked nearby. Five other airmen stood in a small group near the vehicle's open doors. Jack approached them.

"So what do we do?" he asked one of them.

"I guess we just help lift the stretchers into the ambulance when the patients come out. I think it takes about six people to lift one stably."

Jack still wasn't clear on what his role would be in all this, but he stood by patiently. Minutes later, Major Armstrong reappeared.

"Okay, the patients are on their way."

Jack watched as a procession of four or five medical attendants emerged from the doors of the clinic. They swarmed around a single stretcher that bore the form of a human being.

Major Armstrong began directing what followed. "Ok, I need all of the volunteers to gather around."

Jack walked up to the stretcher and took hold of the first handle on the left side. The other five volunteers fell into place as well, three on each side.

"Everyone make sure you have a good grip."

Jack glanced over and looked at the man whom they were about to lift into the ambulance. His eyes stared blankly at the sky, clearly sedated. Stubble dotted his face. His fingernails were stained with blood. A blanket covered most of the soldier's body, but Jack noticed as he and the others were about to lift that the blanket lay flat against the bottom half of the gurney. The soldier had no legs.

"Prepare to lift," Major Armstrong commanded.

"Lift."

The soldier went up and into the vehicle. Attendants were inside the back of the ambulance to secure him. Jack tried to steady the gurney as much as possible, though he felt his arms shaking under the pressure.

"Next."

Another gurney rolled out of the clinic. This soldier was conscious. He wore a neck brace and a cast on one foot. A tattoo of a rosary snaked up his arm. Jack took his position at the front of the stretcher.

"Don't drop me," snarled the soldier.

Up he went, into the back of the ambulance.

Then came another. This one was bad. He had an oxygen bottle and an IV on the stretcher with him. Then another.

Six times the process was repeated.

"Prepare to lift."

"Lift."

Six times Jack wondered what the soldier had been through to get to this point. Six times he wondered what would become of him after today.

When it was over, the ambulance pulled away and Major Armstrong thanked Jack and the others for volunteering. "We appreciate your help," he said, shaking each of their hands, but Jack thought it was odd that he was the one being thanked.

That night, Jack met David Holman and Blake

Davidson at the gym as planned. It wasn't much of a gym, just some weight equipment and a couple of treadmills that had been collected in a spare room at the airfield fire department. Blake loved it here, though, and he cranked his music before immersing himself is a set of bench presses.

David picked up a set of free weights and looked over at Jack, who was climbing aboard a treadmill. "So what did you do over at the clinic, anyway?"

"I don't feel like I did much," said Jack. "They needed help loading some patients into an ambulance, so we helped them."

"Well, that's great of you to volunteer for stuff like that," said David.

Jack shrugged. The whir of the treadmill was picking up pace and he looked down at his feet as he ran. He thought of the soldier who had lost his legs. He thought about how easy it was to take for granted the simple fact that he could run.

8

On the morning of December 20th, Jack was in his CHU strapping his nine-millimeter in place as he got ready to catch the bus. Without warning, an explosion cracked so loudly it felt to Jack as though a semi-truck had overrun the whole billeting compound. Jack instinctively crouched low to take cover. Two more explosions followed in quick succession. His heart raced with the familiar surge of adrenaline and he squeezed his eyes tightly shut as if to push away the sounds that were echoing through his head. The blast rang in his ears for a few seconds. He realized that all was silent outside and that the barrage had apparently been limited to those three rounds. There was no siren to give the all-clear.

After a few moments passed, Jack opened the door of his CHU and stepped outside to look towards the airfield. He saw a wisp of smoke reaching toward the sky where the mortars must have exploded. It looked like it was coming from the main loading ramp, just a few thousand feet away from the CHU compound. They had come close this time. To his left, Jack saw Clark Wilson trudging over the crushed rock pathway, headed toward the bus stop. He jogged over to follow him. "Did you hear that?" Jack asked.

"Of course I did. Do I look like I'm deaf?"

"Well, I think I might be after that explosion. I wonder if anybody was out there when it blew," said Jack, pointing in the direction of the airfield.

"I don't know, but if there was, they're probably long gone by now."

As they approached the road where the bus usually stopped, they saw that several others from their shift had congregated already. Some had been outside when the shells came in. Carl Lee was one of the witnesses, and he wasn't at all shaken by it. "They weren't that close at all," he insisted. "You should have been in Baghdad in '03. We used to get hit a lot worse than this all the time. A couple of little shells like that were no big deal." Everyone else rolled their eyes slightly at his bravado, but weren't willing to challenge him on the veracity of his statement.

Their routine continued as it would have on any other day. They went to the chow hall, got their food and rode back to the Command Post as Blake Davidson sang along to whatever was coming out of the duct-taped dashboard speakers, his amazing aptitude for 70s rock lyrics coming in handy in this desert country. David Holman sat next to Jack on the bus and followed him to the command post when they arrived for their shift.

When they walked into the command post, it became obvious that Cliff Hartman and Jamie Tyndall were swamped with action. Tyndall was talking loudly into the radio receiver and Hartman was holding two telephone handsets, one next to each ear. The load planners, Kathryn Jason and Kelly Shaw, both looked up at Jack as he entered. Kathryn made a made a face that told him things that morning had been busy.

Hartman hung up the phone after a moment and looked at Jack. "Okay," he said. "The airfield has been closed. We already got hit this morning and more attacks are expected throughout the day." Jack nodded.

"What about EOD?" asked David.

"There's an Explosive Ordinance Disposal Team headed out to the airfield in about twenty minutes to do an ordinance sweep. They think that some unexploded mortars could be out there still. Under no conditions do we accept planes in here until we get the all-clear from the Army airfield safety officer."

Jack nodded again and took over the radios from Jamie. Tyndall breathed a sigh of relief as he logged off of the desktop computer. Jack sat down in Jamie's chair and looked over at Hartman again. He could see that the normal energetic squint of the Sergeant's eyes had been drained away by the morning's events.

The phones rang on and off for the first hour of Jack's shift and he calmly multi-tasked and answered each one as efficiently as he could. Captain Garrison completed the accountability checks and determined that all twenty-three Airmen at the Command Post were uninjured. With the airfield closed, there were no cargo missions and the ramp crews huddled in the break room killing time until they could go back to work. They would stay off the ramps until the Army EOD teams completed their sweeps and deemed it safe.

Later that afternoon, Jack went up to the roof with Hans Drago to watch the EOD teams do their work. They could clearly see the armor-suited men as they steered a remote controlled robot into position just in front of the airfield fire department. Jack was glad that he hadn't been at the gym that morning.

"Looks like they found a firecracker," exclaimed Hans. Jack nodded and watched, fixated, as the bomb was slowly deactivated by the metallic arms of the robot. From this vantage point, he could also see the ramp crew heading back outside to move some pallets into the cargo yard. Wayne Parsons was squinting behind the wheel of a forklift as Blake Davidson spotted him into place. The older man's white teeth were showing as he sawed vigorously on the steering wheel.

When the pallet had been successfully moved, Blake turned around and began walking to another load of cargo that they had taken off of a C-130 the night before. Jack extended his hand in the air halfway, as if to raise a mock salute. It caught Blake's eye and he returned the gesture.

"Hey man, we could use your help. Want to come spot for us?"

"Sure, I'll be right down."

Jack clambered down the ladder and walked around the building to the cargo yard. Blake walked over to where Jack was and provided some basic instructions. "Hey, thanks for your help. We're going to be moving these pallets over here with the forklift, just signal when the prongs are in place, okay?" Jack nodded as Blake jumped into the driver's seat of an extra forklift. The engine sputtered to life and the machine began to roll.

Inside the command post, David Holman was working on an after-action report for the attacks that morning. Despite the air-conditioner that rattled in the window, it was hot and stuffy. He got up and walked into the break room. The refrigerator was pleasantly cool and he took a swig of water from a freshly-opened bottle. It felt good as the moisture hit his raspy throat.

As he tipped the bottle a little higher to pour the last drop into his mouth, the attack sirens echoed again with their familiar warning. "ROCKET ATTCK, ROCKET

ATTACK." Another huge blast shook the walls of the command post. Hans Drago had been on the roof when the warning was sounded. He threw open the door to the command post and ran the length of the hallway. "Get down," he screamed.

Several more rockets made their presence known and everyone inside the building seemed to simultaneously duck under any solid piece of furniture they could find. David threw himself under the break room's large wooden table in a singular diving movement. Storage shelves filled with food items tipped from the jarring explosions outside, dumping their contents on the tabletop that was shielding David's head.

From under the table, David could look directly across the hallway at Kelly Shaw and Tony Graham as they both crouched under desks in the map room. Dust seemed to stream down from the ceiling and swirl in the air like they were in a full-fledged dust storm. Soon the density of the cloudy particles blocked them from David's sight completely. More explosions could be heard outside. It was a long time before the all-clear message was relayed.

When it was over, Captain Garrison walked into the break room. "Everyone ok?" he asked. David nodded as he dusted himself off.

"I think we're good, sir."

"All right. I'm putting you in charge of another round of accountability. Let me know when you've checked up on everyone."

"Will do, sir," replied David. He was heading back toward his work area across the hall when Blake Davidson stopped him in his tracks. Blake's face was dusty and his eyed were red.

"Holman. Did you see Jack?"

"No, where is he?"

"I think he's gone."

"Where could he have gone, wasn't he just outside with you?"

"No, I mean I think he's *gone*. We need to call medical."

David stared at Blake for a second as he felt his senses go numb. He would have few recollections of the rest of that day. He would have no memory of calling mortuary affairs. He wouldn't remember completing the casualty report. After seeing the red bloodstain on the ground where Jack had fallen, the only thing that would register in David's mind was the fact that Jack was indeed gone.

9

The next day, the phone rang while David was on shift at the Command Post. Kathryn Jason answered it. She listened to the voice on the other end of the line and jotted a few notes. After hanging up, she turned and looked at Staff Sergeant Shaw. "Jack's HR mission is ready. They'll be here shortly with the casket."

David had seen three other HR flights since he had been at Sherman, evacuating the "human remains" of Army troops killed in action. The others he'd witnessed had been somber enough. The casualty would be brought to the ramp in an American flag-draped coffin, unloaded from the Army's mortuary affairs hearse and transferred to the cargo bay of a specially-assigned C-130 for the final flight home. All personnel in sight of the plane would snap to attention as a chaplain or commander said something in a brief ceremony about the individual's sacrifice and dedication. This one was different, though. Everyone had known Jack. His loss made the thought of this HR flight a nauseating experience. Every time David's mind went back to yesterday, he winced at the thought of the grief that was winding its way back around the world.

Barely half an hour after SSgt Jason got the initial notification, a C-130 was touching down on the runway. It would not take off again until Jack's body was onboard.

Dusk was setting in as the plane taxied to a stop on the main loading ramp just outside of the command post building. Tony Graham and David Holman took one of the white Dodges out to the plane as the rest of the loading crew followed to wait for the mortuary affairs convoy.

David didn't know exactly how long it would take for the procession to arrive, so he climbed aboard the C-130 to brief the pilot and crew on the situation. The mission's loadmaster responded on behalf of the others. "Roger that," he said. They had no schedule to keep and no mission objective except to transfer the remains of the fallen airman with dignity. The loadmaster outlined their itinerary to prove his point, explaining that they would fly directly back to their base in Kuwait that night. From there, the casket would be transferred onto a C-17 and flown to Germany before finally being returned to the United States through Dover AFB, Delaware. The crew understood the situation and said that the possibility of a delay was no problem.

After exiting the plane, David walked back to the truck and climbed into the passenger's seat to wait for the vehicles to arrive. Tony Graham sat silently in front of the wheel. Twenty minutes passed and David could feel the gravity of what was about to happen physically bearing down on him. His mind was swirling with questions about Jack. He turned to Tony.

"I still don't know why he had to be out there just then."

"Who, Jack?"

"Yes."

"Well, there was no way of knowing."

David paused. The truck was silent again.

"Yeah, but it just doesn't make sense. None of this

makes sense."

Tony looked at him. "Well, that's war for you, I guess."

"I guess you're right."

Dusk faded into a clear, crisp night as they sat there, waiting to see the headlights of the convoy turn onto the ramp. There was nothing else to say.

When they finally came, the two yellow beams of the lead truck were prominently visible as it headed up a line of a half-dozen vehicles. David watched, expecting them to turn right and make their way from the taxi area to the loading ramp. To his astonishment, the trucks kept on rolling straight ahead and wheeled out onto the active runway. Operations were still taking place even in the darkness of the night and several unmanned drones were preparing for their final approach. David had the handheld radio set with him that could put him in touch with the Air Traffic Control Tower. He keyed the microphone and asked the controller if the string of vehicles had received clearance to proceed onto the active runway.

"Negative, negative. The trucks are not cleared for entry onto the active runway." David was shocked by the reply.

"Should we do something?" He looked at Tony Graham, who had been listening to the exchange from the driver's seat.

"I don't think we have much of a choice."

"Let's go."

The words hadn't even cleared his tongue when Tony threw the truck in gear and whipped the steering wheel to the left. He guided the truck off the concrete pad of the loading ramp, committing its tires to weeds and sand. He gunned the motor and they charged over the terrain, cutting across the airfield to get to the runway where the trucks were still oblivious to what was happening. Tony was absolutely focused, staring at every cranny and ground divot their headlights revealed as he pushed the speedometer up to forty, fifty, and then sixty miles per hour. The Dodge creaked and grumbled, hitting every hole and bump with increasing force. David looked back and could see the landing lights of a UAV closing in the distance and knew that they'd be cutting time very close if they even made it to the convoy at all. They continued to fly across the landscape, churning up a plume of dust that chased them the whole way as the runway strip grew larger and larger in the windshield.

Tony knew what he was doing behind the wheel and David was thankful. He dropped their speed to about thirty miles per hour and made a hard right turn to bring their truck parallel with the convoy. Then he rolled down his side window and waved his arm outside to get the lead driver's attention. The Army trucker slowed to a stop and looked at Tony with a blank expression. From David's vantage point, the driver appeared to be an E-2 Private. "You need to get off of this runway," said Tony. "It's active and there's going to be a UAV landing here any second."

"We're going out to where the C-130 is parked with HR," replied the truck driver.

Tony raised his voice even louder. "Well, you missed it. Turn around and
 follow me."

He rolled up the window and gunned the engine again. He put the truck into a one-eighty spin and ran it parallel to the runway in the opposite direction. Up ahead were the ever-looming lights of the UAV speeding in their direction head-on. Tony turned onto the taxiway leading back to the loading ramp just in time for the convoy to follow safely. They cleared the runway before the UAV made its landing with few seconds to spare.

Tony coasted at low speed and brought the truck to a stop a few hundred yards from the back of the C-130. The temporary diversion from the real reason he and David were there dissolved as soon as they saw the somber faces of the ramp crew at attention. The convoy of four or five vehicles rolled to a stop behind them as Tony and David got out of the truck and discreetly joined the ranks of the makeshift honor guard that had formed in two single-file lines to create a pathway leading from the concrete tarmac to the back of the C-130.

Captain Garrison got out of the second truck and quietly whispered a few commands of instruction to them as the hearse backed into place. It wasn't a hearse like those used at civilian funerals. This was more of a pickup with a special cap attached to the back of it. Wayne Parsons and Clark Wilson opened the doors on the back of the cap to reveal a simple metal coffin, draped with an American flag. Those in line stood silently at attention as they slowly removed the casket from the back of the vehicle.

As the casket passed slowly in front of them, David and the others snapped in unison to a salute of reverence and then filed in line behind the casket as it was delicately carried up the loading ramp of the C-130 and placed in the cargo bay. They gathered around the inside of the aircraft. Captain Garrison looked at David.

"Sergeant Holman?" he asked. "Would you like to say anything?"

David had not planned on eulogizing his friend, and Garrison's offer caught him off guard. A lump swelled in his thought as he thought for a few moments.

"I don't know what can be said at a time like this. Maybe the Twenty-Third Psalm would be appropriate." As David began, the words came out slowly. The others soon joined in.

10

David's last days at FOB Sherman went by in a blur. Since Jack's death, he'd gone about his duties with a sullen detachment and he wanted nothing except to be home with this experience behind him. The duty schedule had been altered to cover for Jack's place, with David and Jamie Tyndall alternating twelve-hour shifts. Jack's loss had left a surreal void in the command post's working dynamic. The airmen kept their thoughts to themselves, working steadily and the work seemed more tedious than ever. David was mentally counting off each day that remained. It seemed like torture, water dripping slowly from the end of a pipe, minutes seeming to take hours.

On the last day, David didn't know when he woke up that he would leave FOB Sherman by nightfall. As a result, he failed to make a mental note of his last trip to the chow hall and the final bus ride to the Command Post that followed. The day itself was hazy, and it seemed as though the whole base was cloaked in a fog-like combination of dust and smoke that flowed from the giant burn pit that the army used to incinerate trash. Its stinking odor seemed to latch onto everything and everyone as if it was misty, smoky glue.

At work, David's replacement, Sergeant Jerry Baylor, was sitting at the desk and handling most of the radio calls. At this point, Baylor was already confident with the radio receiver. He was experienced, and David knew that he would be leaving his shift in good hands.

"David, take a look at this." Baylor was working on the next day's flying schedule and had already handled the afternoon weather dispatches with perfection. He showed David the forecasts, all of which indicated that the dust storm would thicken by nightfall, blocking out all possibility of air travel for the next few days. "Doesn't look good," he said. "Looks like you might be stuck here for a bit longer than you expected. David nodded. "I don't like the sound of that."

Captain Garrison walked into the command post and David explained the situation to him. 'I see," he said. The captain was silent for at least a moment and spent that time studying the weather reports. Finally, he spoke, his words spilling over with their usual almost-southern accent. "Sergeant Holman, I don't like the idea of you leaving before your replacements get their full three-day turnover, but I see your point. Why don't you go back to your CHU and get your gear cleared out."

David looked at him and replied with a little hesitation. "So I can leave today?" Garrison relaxed his stance and put his hand on his hip. "Well, I don't know what we've got going out of here aircraft-wise, but if you and Sergeant Hartman and Airman Tyndall can find a plane that's headed to Qatar, you're free to go. You've completed your mission here."

David smiled. "Copy that, sir." He excused himself from the command post and walked down the hall to the break room where Jamie Tyndall was asleep on one of the couches. David kicked the padded cushion nearest his head and watched as Jamie's eyes twitched open a few times. "Hey, Garrison said we can get out of here tonight if we can catch a plane." Jamie grunted and started to sit up. "Huh?"

"Garrison said we're released. Get your gear packed up."

Jamie blinked his eyes a couple times, then got up from the couch and followed David out the door. They both climbed into one of the pickups and started back to the billeting compound. Back at the CHUs, David got busy stuffing gear into his duffle bags while Jamie futilely tried to sweep the dust off the floor and out of the CHU altogether. It had accumulated like a fine layer of snow over most of the furnishings and gear that hadn't been regularly used or cleaned over the past six months. Cursing under his breath, he eventually gave up and started sorting through his own personal items. Within a few minutes, he had a plastic bag full of toiletries, clothing items, magazines and food that David wondered if he was going to throw away. "Hey, are you going to trash all that stuff?" he asked.

"Yep. Plan on travelling light."

It was a good point. David re-evaluated what would be necessary for his own trip back to the States and added a few pairs of socks and some magazines to the trash bag's contents. With their bags full and their living quarters empty, David Holman and Jamie Tyndall closed the door behind them for the last time and threw their gear into the back of the truck. David had two duffle bags, each about three-quarters full, and Tyndall had one that was packed so tightly it looked like the seams were about to give way. They drove back through the Ugandan checkpoint where a guard named met them and extended his hand, signaling for them to bring the pickup to a halt.

"Jambo," he said.

"Jambo," David replied, displaying his ID card. "Good to go," replied the guard, giving the Americans the thumbs-up sign. "We're going home tonight," yelled Jamie as they pulled away. The Ugandan did not share his enthusiasm, and David watched as his smile turned to a look of puzzlement in the rear view mirror.

Within seconds, they were parking in front of the Command Post. David entered the radio room where Sergeant Baylor and Cliff Hartman's replacement, Sergeant Cortez, were sitting. A movie was playing on the TV screen on the wall.

Sergeant Baylor looked at David. "All set to leave?" he asked.

"Are you kidding? I've been ready to go for the last six months."

Turning to the computer screen at what used to be his work station, Jamie Tyndall asked Baylor if any airlift missions were still on the schedule for that night. "Yeah, there's one", he said. "A C-17, due in at about 22:00 local time. It might get canceled though, because of the dust." David nodded. "Well, if it does come in, we're going to try to get on it." He pointed to Jamie, who was standing in the doorway. "Make sure it's going to Qatar," he added.

"It is," said Baylor. "I'll let you know if anything changes."

"Great. I'll be in the break room. I'm going to try to get some rest."

David sat down on one of the couches and closed his eyes, but the excitement he felt did not let it come easily. He thought of Kristine and smiled at the idea of sleeping in their own bed in just a few more days.

David awoke to Baylor's radio call that the C-17 was

inbound and ten minutes out. He sat up and caught a glimpse of Tyndall racing by the doorway. He grabbed his boonie hat and got up, following Tyndall down the hallway for the last time. Holman stopped and said goodbye to Baylor and Cortez. Captain Garrison shook both their hands as David and Jamie strapped on their body armor. "See ya'll in Al Udeid," he said. Garrison's replacement was due in any day, after which he would be on his way home as well.

David looked back at the bullet holes that marked the walls like chicken pox, remembering the first time he'd stepped into the building six months earlier. He thought of Jack Doolittle's enthusiasm that night and wished that he had been able to enjoy the trip home. He gave Captain Garrison a final goodbye, looked at Tyndall and said it was time to go. They walked past the mural of the Iraqi eagle on their way to the truck. David climbed in the back with their gear as Tyndall called shotgun. One of the new ramp loaders had volunteered to drive them out to the aircraft. Davidson had already left, the day before. They rolled off and left the Command Post behind for good.

Ten minutes later, the C-17 touched down and began its taxi to the ramp where they were waiting. It had minimal cargo onboard, so the offload was completed quickly by one forklift. To David, the green lights on each of the plane's wings strobed with a particularly entrancing glow.

They walked up to the back of the plane and identified the crew's loadmaster, conspicuous in his headset and tan flight suit. Tyndall asked him if they could spare enough room on the plane for two passengers who needed to get to Qatar. He looked at David and then back at Jamie suspiciously and said "Nahh, I think we're pretty full."

David glanced up at the empty cargo bay of the aircraft and then at the loadmaster's stripes. He was a Technical Sergeant.

"Really?" Jamie asked, obviously irritated. "We've been here for over six months. We talk to you guys all the time on the radios, and we'd kinda like to get home."

The loadmaster looked them over again, paused for a moment and said, "All right, you can sit up on the flight deck with the rest of the crew. We still don't have any room in the bay."

"Sounds good," said David.

They both charged onto the loading ramp of the C-17 and made their way up the short ladder that led to the aircraft's flight deck. David turned and looked behind him one last time to see the large cargo door closing behind them. He could glimpse just a bit of quickly disappearing concrete and made a mental note of it as his final memory of FOB Sherman. He climbed the rest of the way up the ladder and was suddenly in the midst of the aircrew's flight deck.

Directly in front of Jamie was the massive windscreen which framed the entire cockpit with Plexiglas. A multitude of buttons, switches and dials surrounded the pilot and copilot, who sat in identical seats. Behind them were two jump seats that the loadmaster motioned to. Jamie looked at David with amazement. They both sat down and buckled in.

Soon the sound of four turbocharged engines pierced David's eardrums. It was followed by the sensation of slow, gradual movement. They had begun their taxi and within minutes, they would be airborne and on their way home.

The flight was smooth and David dozed off shortly after the landing gear came up. The next thing he remembered was the pilot reaching over and tapping him on the shoulder.

"Hey, check this out," he said.

David leaned around from his chair and looked out the windscreen just as the pilot eased the aircraft into a gradual bank that put the lights of a major city directly below them.

"That's Baghdad."

David did a double take as he took in the splendor of the city's lights. To him, the lights were so majestic and beautiful that it was hard to believe they represented a city whose name had become synonymous with turmoil. David couldn't tell exactly how high they were, but they were close enough to the ground that he could easily make out the silhouettes of buildings and homes as they passed overhead. Radio and television antennas popped up from many of the roofs and the lights that flickered from streetlights and windows seemed to glow like the electric bulbs of a Christmas tree. David tried to burn the image of that city into his mind forever.

"I don't think I'll ever forget this ride," he said to the Captain. The Captain smiled, unused to amazement at what was to him at least a weekly sight.

For the rest of the flight, David sat back in his seat and relaxed. Jamie snored in the chair next to him for at least an hour or two, his head bouncing up and down every time the aircraft hit a patch of turbulence, smacking his chin against his flak jacket.

When they landed at Al Udeid, it was early in the daylight hours. Though the base was still shrouded with the same distinct smell that David remembered from six months earlier, it wasn't unpleasant this time. Now that smell reminded him that he was one stop closer to home.

The loadmaster that they had bargained with the night before caught up to them as they were walking down the loading platform for the last time.

"Hey guys," he said. "Just a quick heads-up here, but you might want to lay low for a while before you check in with the Personnel desk. You weren't manifested or anything and they probably won't like that there."

The two airmen nodded at him in thanks and walked off the tarmac. The only way to leave the flight line was through the PERSCO tent.

Jack and Jamie weren't sure what the loadmaster was talking about, but they told the airman at the check-in counter that their flight information had blown away, just to be safe. She gave them each a ticket with a tent number on it and said that they were to check in every day before noon to receive updates on their final departure time for home. It would be at least three or four days until they heard anything.

Within an hour, David had gotten clean bed sheets from the issue tent, stowed away his gear and got started on a nap which ended up lasting about fifteen hours. He was tired, and after more than six months in a combat zone without a day off, it felt great to let his mind rest for a while.

When he woke up the next day, it was already mid-morning. Streams of blinding light invaded the tent through cracks at the corners and bottoms of its fabric walls. David looked around the inside and saw the rows of bunk beds reverberating with the snores of several dozen troops still asleep. Jamie was heading off to the gym, but David was in no mood to tag along. Instead, he leisurely got up, showered, and grabbed breakfast at the chow hall.

On the way back to the tent, he ran into Jamie, who

was just getting ready to head to the morale tent.

"Want to come?" asked Jamie.

"Sure, why not?"

The morale tent was a huge canopy that resembled a circus big-top. Tables and chairs were set up under the canopy facing a stage which was flanked by two enormous fans. The stage itself was sandstone, decorated with zigzag patterns that gave it a distinctively middle-eastern appearance. Two guitarists in Air Force PT uniforms sat front and center. One was busy hitting mellow chords on an electric guitar while the other plucked on his bass.

Jamie said he had met some girls earlier who promised to be here around this time, and he desperately glanced around at the various faces that occupied the chairs directly in front of the stage. When he spotted them, he was gone from David's field of vision almost instantly. David had to turn around and try very hard to pick him out from the crowd in order to see him darting over to the girls' table.

David opted to focus on the music and the atmosphere instead but soon realized that his evening would be more enjoyable if he returned to billeting. He went for a walk around the billeting area's "tent city". The shelters were all dark and quiet. They looked invitingly peaceful, and David soon found himself entering his own to reacquaint himself with his bunk.

When he awoke the next morning, Jamie Tyndall was packing his bags. "We're leaving at 1800 tonight," he mumbled.

David turned around and looked at him.

"Really?" he asked.

"Yeah, that's what I said."

"Did you go to PERSCO?"

Jamie looked at David with ridicule. "Where else would I find out our flight time?" David didn't understand why he was so touchy this morning, but he paid it no mind and rose to shower, shave, and get his things together as well.

Although their flight time was at 1800 hours, they had to be ready well in advance to turn in the body armor, helmets and ammunition that had been issued to them on their way in-theater. The whole out-processing business would take about four hours to complete, so they showed up at PERSCO early in the afternoon to allow plenty of time.

Just as predicted, David was sitting in one of the back rows of a commercial airliner four hours later. Jamie was somewhere up in the front of the plane and between them were about eighty marines and airmen, all equally ready to set foot on American soil once again. It was a long flight back and David tried to sleep through as much of it as he could. There was a brief refueling stop in Germany, but unlike the trip over, there was no off-base layover this time.

In Baltimore, David got off the chartered airliner with little fanfare and embraced the civilian world of America once again. He felt vulnerable and conspicuous in his uniform and tried to avoid the glances of travelers that seemed to converge on him from every direction. An elderly man with a US Navy hat extended his hand as David walked by him on an escalator and said "Welcome home, son." David smiled graciously, but would have rather deflected the attention altogether.

At the ticket counter, a lady told him that he was to catch a connection flight into Detroit within an hour, so David had to hurry to the other side of the airport to meet the plane at its gate. He called Kristine on a pay phone and told her he'd be home soon. She promised to meet him in Detroit.

When the plane finally touched down in Detroit, David picked up his carry-on bag and followed the rest of the passengers down the walkway. His heart raced as he thought about Kristine and the world he had left six months earlier.

The final doorway was approaching quickly and David closed his eyes as he ducked through the last portal between him and home. There she was. Her hands were clasped tightly in front of her in anticipation. She smiled like David had never seen her smile before, but the spark of joy in her eyes was wonderfully familiar. He took Kristine in his arms and with the warmth of that embrace; he knew that his war was finally over.

GLOSSARY

ABU: Airman's Battle Uniform

CHU: Containerized Housing Unit

DFAC: Dining Facility

A1C: Airman 1st Class (E-3)

FOB: Forward Operating Base

PFC: Private First Class

PT: Physical Training

Republican Guard: Elite corps of Saddam Hussein's Iraqi military that were used primarily as Special Forces and dictatorial body guards.

SrA: Senior Airman (E-4)

SSgt: Staff Sergeant (Air Force: E-5, Army: E-6)

TSgt: Technical Sergeant (E-6)

UAV: Unmanned Aerial Vehicle

ABOUT THE AUTHOR

Andrew Layton is an Air Force veteran of the wars in Iraq and Afghanistan. In 2010, he was involved in launching the first humanitarian airlift missions into earthquake-ravaged Haiti. His other books include the nonfiction works *Eagles' Wings: An Uncommon Story of World War II* and *Wolverines in the Sky: Michigan's Fighter Aces of WWI, WWII and Korea*. Layton holds a B.A. in Political Science from Albion College and lives with his wife Elise in Battle Creek, Michigan.